"Mari? Theo?

Sam's voice was a welcome relief. Yet Mari didn't move out from their hiding spot. For all she knew, the gunman was hiding inside somewhere, waiting to take one last shot.

"We're okay!" she shouted as loudly as she could. "We're hiding!" She didn't know how much to say in case the gunman was listening.

"Stay where you are!" Sam called.

She didn't respond, hoping the gunman would figure out that he was about to get caught. If he was hiding inside the house.

Her ex-husband, Roy? Or someone else? That was the tough question.

"Mommy? Is that Mr. Sam?" Theo asked with a loud sniffle.

"Yes." She glanced down at her son. "He's going to make sure we're safe. He won't let the scary man find us."

"I like Mr. Sam," Theo whispered.

His innocent words made her chest tighten. She was happy Theo had someone to look up to, but it was so wrong that her young son was scared out of his mind.

Laura Scott has always loved romance and read faith-based books by Grace Livingston Hill in her teenage years. She's thrilled to have been given the opportunity to retire from thirty-eight years of nursing to become a full-time author. Laura has published over thirty books for Love Inspired Suspense. She has two adult children and lives in Milwaukee, Wisconsin, with her husband of thirty-five years. Please visit Laura at laurascottbooks.com, as she loves to hear from her readers.

Books by Laura Scott

Love Inspired Suspense

Hiding in Plain Sight
Amish Holiday Vendetta
Deadly Amish Abduction
Tracked Through the Woods
Kidnapping Cold Case
Guarding His Secret Son

Justice Seekers

Soldier's Christmas Secrets
Guarded by the Soldier
Wyoming Mountain Escape
Hiding His Holiday Witness
Rocky Mountain Standoff
Fugitive Hunt

Mountain Country K-9 Unit

Baby Protection Mission

Texas Justice

Texas Kidnapping Target

Visit the Author Profile page at LoveInspired.com for more titles.

Texas Kidnapping Target

LAURA SCOTT

LOVE INSPIRED SUSPENSE

INSPIRATIONAL ROMANCE

LOVE INSPIRED®SUSPENSE
INSPIRATIONAL ROMANCE

Recycling programs
for this product may
not exist in your area.

ISBN-13: 978-1-335-63846-5

Texas Kidnapping Target

Love Inspired
22 Adelaide St. West, 41st Floor
Toronto, Ontario M5H 4E3, Canada
www.LoveInspired.com

Printed in Lithuania

MIX
Paper | Supporting
responsible forestry
FSC® C021394

In whom we have redemption through his blood,
even the forgiveness of sins.
—*Colossians* 1:14

This book is dedicated to my wonderful
critique group. Thanks for all the brainstorming help!

ONE

A soft cry brought Mari Lynch instantly awake. Heart thudding, she strained to listen. Silence. Was Theo having a nightmare?

She slid out of bed, the hardwood floor icy cold beneath her bare feet. She grabbed the 12-gauge shotgun leaning next to her bed. Wearing nothing but her flannel pajamas, she hurried down the hall to her four-year-old son's room.

"Mommy!"

Theo's cry had her wrenching the door open. A blast of cold air hit her face. She gasped at the sight of a masked man looming over her son's bed, reaching for Theo.

"Stop or I'll shoot!"

Instantly, the intruder spun away from the boy, ducked back out the window and took off at a sprint. She wanted to fire the gun but couldn't make herself pull the trigger. Darting toward the open window, she aimed the barrel of the shotgun at his disappearing shadow. Seconds later, he vanished behind the barn.

"Theo!" She turned toward her son. He jumped off his bed and launched himself at her still holding his favorite stuffed dog, Charlie to his chest. She caught him close, her heart hammering against her ribs.

What was going on? Who had tried to kidnap her son?

She belatedly noticed the window was completely gone. It took her a moment to understand the intruder had used a glass cutter to access the house.

Her house! To get her son!

Whirling away from the open window, she took Theo from the room, slamming the door shut behind her. Then hurried to the kitchen to call 911. Her Whistling Creek Ranch was twenty miles outside of Fredericksburg, so she didn't anticipate a quick response.

But she needed to report this to the police.

Mari wished she'd reported the stranger she'd glimpsed walking the tree line of her property last night, too. Likely the same man who'd just tried to grab her son, although he hadn't been wearing a ski mask. She'd reached for her shotgun then too, but by the time she'd returned to the window, he was gone.

He must have been casing her house. Figuring

out which window was Theo's. But why attempt to kidnap her son?

After the dispatcher promised to send Deputy Strawn to the ranch, she carried Theo into her room. She quickly changed into jeans and a warm forest green sweater. She stuffed her feet into work boots in case she needed to head outside.

"Who was that scary man?" Theo had calmed down a bit, still gripping his stuffed dog Charlie tightly.

"I don't know, sweetheart." She wasn't sure what to say. How to explain to her son what was really going on here. She didn't want to frighten him. "Maybe he was lost. Or was homeless and wanted a place to stay."

"He told me to come wif him." Theo gazed at her from wide, blue eyes. "I didn't wanna go."

Her mouth went dry with fear and she silently prayed her ex-husband hadn't sent someone after their son. But who else would do such a thing? Her last, extremely tense meeting with Roy flashed in her mind.

She scooped Theo up and carried him into the living room. She needed to get that window boarded up, as soon as possible. Maybe Deputy Strawn would keep watch outside while she managed that task.

Christmas tree lights brightened the room. The New Year holiday was only five days away, and

Theo had asked if they could keep the tree up longer. All the way to his birthday, on January 2.

Setting Theo down on the sofa, she took a moment to feed split logs into the wood-burning stove to combat the cold air seeping from Theo's room. When she turned back to her son, the sight of a black SUV pulling up to the house caught her eye.

The intruder?

She dashed into her room, grabbed the shotgun and returned to the living room. She hovered along the wall close to the large picture window overlooking her front yard.

A man wearing a Stetson slid out from behind the wheel to stand next to the SUV. It was too soon for Deputy Strawn to show up—she'd barely made the call five minutes ago. Was this a trick? A way to force her to drop her guard? The guy blatantly stared at her house, without any attempt to be subtle.

Anger spurred her forward. "Stay on the sofa, Theo."

"Okay, Mommy."

She flung the front door open and stepped out onto the covered porch, the top eves decorated with Christmas lights. She lifted the shotgun to her shoulder and aimed the barrel squarely at the intruder's chest. "Do not come any closer. Turn around, get back in your car and drive away."

He froze, lifting his hands in a gesture of surrender. A glint of silver caught her eye. He wore a silver star on his chest. He was a lawman, a Texas Ranger, not someone associated with Roy. Yet she didn't relax. He'd gotten here too quickly for her piece of mind.

"Ma'am, I'm Ranger Sam Hayward. Will you please put the gun down?"

"Why are you here?" She did not lower the weapon one iota.

He wasn't too far away that she couldn't see the way his eyebrow arched upward at her less than welcoming tone. "I want to ask you a few questions, that's all."

"At this hour? It's eleven o'clock at night." She paused, then asked, "Did the sheriff's department send you?"

"What? No." He looked startled by her question. "I just need to talk to you."

"Come back tomorrow."

Again he looked surprised. "Ma'am, please. I'm not here to hurt you. Quite the opposite." He paused. "I would really appreciate if y'all would lower that shotgun."

They stared at each other for a long second. With a sigh, she lowered the weapon. She couldn't continue standing here, leaving Theo unprotected in case the assailant decided to return. "Fine. Come inside."

"Thank you, ma'am." He gave her a nod, mounted the steps to the porch then entered her house. He looked around curiously, his gaze landing on Theo, who was thankfully still curled up in the corner of the couch.

She didn't offer him a seat or anything to drink. Setting the shotgun aside, she crossed her arms over her chest. "What is this about?"

"Have you seen your ex-husband?"

Her stomach clenched as her worst fears were realized. "No. He's in prison. There would be visitor logs that would prove I have not been to see him since our divorce two years ago." A divorce that had become final shortly after Roy was found guilty of murder by a jury of his peers and subsequently incarcerated for life, without the possibility of parole.

Ranger Hayward held her gaze for a long moment. "Roy Carlton isn't in jail. He escaped."

What? Her heart lodged in her throat, making it impossible to speak. To breathe. Theo! Had Roy tried to kidnap their son?

No! Please, Lord Jesus, no!

"When?" Her voice was little more than a croak. This couldn't be happening.

"He was declared missing over ninety minutes ago." The ranger's mouth thinned. "He managed to escape from the hospital while apparently faking an illness."

Her mouth opened, but no words came out.

"You have every right to be angry," he said with a slight nod. "This shouldn't have happened. That's why I'm here. I wanted to check in on you and your son. Also to ask if you have any idea where your ex-husband might be hiding."

The words hammered into her brain like nails into a barn door. She managed to pull herself together. "I think he was here a few minutes ago. A man wearing a ski mask cut through the glass in Theo's room and tried to grab him."

"Here?" The ranger's eyes widened. "Show me."

She scooped Theo and Charlie into her arms and led the way down the hall to her son's room. She pushed the door open and gestured for him to go in. "He cut the glass on the window."

"I need to search the property." The ranger glanced at her with concern. "Will you be okay here for a few minutes?"

"Yes, but you should know I saw a man outside the ranch house yesterday evening, too. Not close, near the tree line."

His expression was grim. "Stay inside and keep that shotgun handy."

She forced a nod, her thoughts spinning like a tornado.

Roy had escaped. She and Theo were in danger.

Her nightmare was far from over. The real terror had just begun.

* * *

Sam turned and headed outside. He couldn't believe Roy had gotten to the Whistling Creek so fast! The escaped convict must have had a ride waiting for him. He wished he and his fellow rangers, Jackson Woodlow, Marshall Branson and Tucker Powell, hadn't spent so much time searching around the hospital campus for Roy Carlton. After thirty minutes of finding nothing, he'd left them to it, taking the responsibility to head out to the ranch.

Having Carlton's ex-wife step outside with a shotgun leveled at his chest had been unexpected. Granted most Texans owned guns, but she'd surprised him. Oddly, he respected her for it.

And better understood her hostility after learning about the attempted abduction of her son.

He left the house via the front door, then headed toward the back of the ranch house to scour the area around her son's window. Using his flashlight, he peered at the ground. There were overlapping footprints in the snow and mud. Nothing useful.

He turned to sweep the area. To his surprise, Ms. Lynch leaned out the window. "He disappeared behind the barn."

"Understood." He crossed toward the outbuilding. The barn was long but apparently empty as he could see the herd of cattle gathered near a lean-to shelter.

He took his time, making sure no one was hiding inside the barn, or anywhere nearby. It was likely Carlton had fled the area, but he needed to be sure.

As he worked on clearing the immediate area around the house, he wondered if the would-be kidnapper was really Roy Carlton, or someone else. Carlton had help getting away from the hospital, that much was for sure. But ninety minutes wasn't a lot of time for Roy to have escaped, gotten a change of clothes and a ride to reach the Whistling Creek ranch in time to snatch the kid.

Carlton could have arranged for his accomplice to do the deed. The prosecutor on the case didn't believe Roy had acted alone in the murder of Austin City Manager Hank George.

Unfortunately, Carlton hadn't named anyone else as being involved. Not even in exchange for a lighter sentence.

And truthfully, Roy Carlton struck him as the kind of guy who wouldn't hesitate to do just that.

Then again, Carlton had left his DNA at the scene of the crime. His attempt to ditch the gun hadn't worked either. The weapon had been found in a dumpster a few blocks from the location of George's body and Carlton's fingerprints had been found on the handle. The combination of the two critical pieces of evidence had ensured a swift and just guilty verdict from the jury.

Sam focused on the immediate threat. Once he'd cleared the area around the house, and poked his head inside the barn and chicken coop, he widened his search radius. Unfortunately, the Whistling Creek property was large and spacious. Frustrating to admit Carlton could be hiding anywhere in the woods, despite the frigid temps.

He spied a long row of hay spread out along the short side of the barn for the cattle to eat during the winter. He crossed over, kicking at several clumps to make sure nobody was hiding beneath it.

He didn't find anything. Bypassing the rest of the open pasture area, he headed for the line of trees. He slowed his pace, inspecting the area closely for signs someone had been there.

And there it was. A broken twig. Another one a few feet away. He continued following the faint trail, the ground softer here, somewhat protected by the trees. Was this the path Carlton had taken? Or the intruder Ms. Lynch had seen the previous night?

Could they be one and the same? If so, the kidnapper wasn't Carlton as he escaped two hours ago.

For a few yards he didn't see anything. Just

as he was about to stop and backtrack, he found what he was looking for.

Another partial heel print, the rounded area indicating the assailant had moved farther away from the ranch house.

For a moment he hesitated. Was he following the right trail? This area of the ranch was rather remote, and he couldn't say for sure the tracks he'd found belonged to the assailant who'd tried to kidnap Ms. Lynch's son.

He scowled and turned to look behind him. He'd gone so far that he could no longer see the ranch house. Just the side of the barn where the hay was kept.

Sam stood for a long moment, listening as the wind rustled the trees. The sound of water trickling along a rocky bed reached his ears. From Whistling Creek?

He moved closer, scanning the woods for anyone lurking nearby. Mari Lynch hadn't mentioned the intruder carrying a gun, but almost everyone in Texas had one, which meant he could easily have the business end of a rifle pointed directly at him as he moved through the woods.

Finding the creek, he paused and listened again. Despite the freezing temperatures, there was a still a bit of water trickling along the rocky bed. If this cold snap continued, he figured the creek would freeze over before long.

Around here, the temperatures warmed during the day especially when the sun was out. He was about to turn away, when a dark shape caught his eye.

It almost looked as if a garbage bag was stuck between the ground and some bushes along the creek. Too small to be a person. Dismissing it as a non-threat, he kept going. He needed to keep searching Mari's property, to make sure Carlton wasn't hiding somewhere.

He took his time scouring the ground. Either he was losing his touch or the intruder hadn't come up this way.

He preferred to believe it was the latter.

Sam lengthened his stride to cover the ground more quickly. If the intruder had been here, there was no sign of him now. Either because he was hiding deeper on the ranch property, or because he'd angled off in another direction, joining an accomplice.

Throwing one leg, then the other over the plank fencing around the pasture, he approached the barn. Several of the cows turned wide, placid faces in his direction, apparently curious. Playing his light along the ground, he noted it was muddy here in the pasture. Well, mud mixed with cow pies. The scent was pungent. Cattle hooves had churned up the ground, especially near a large water trough.

No human footprints from what he could see, although they would have been easy to hide in this mess.

It was years since he'd been on a ranch. He came from a family of lawmen, starting with his granddad, his father and now him. But his high school friend Cameron had worked a ranch, and Sam had spent more than enough time there to learn the ropes.

He didn't miss it, not really. But he hadn't minded those summers working outside with the livestock either.

As much as he wanted to head back up to the ranch house, he hesitated. The garbage bag at the creek nagged at him.

He should have checked it out. It didn't seem possible Roy Carlton or anyone else had used it as a hiding spot. The bag had likely been left behind by kids using the creek as a place to hang out. Thoughtful of them to gather their garbage together. Even as that thought entered his head, he realized that wasn't likely. Since when did teenagers clean up after themselves?

Since never.

Moving quickly, he turned and jogged down to the patch of trees. He spotted the large black garbage bag again, on the opposite side of the creek. Stepping carefully on the slippery rocks, he crossed the water.

Footprints, several of them, immediately caught his attention. He still thought it was likely kids, but as he grew closer, it was obvious that there were only two sets of footprints.

One larger, and one smaller.

Moving cautiously now, he approached the garbage bag. As before, he stared at it for a long time. It never moved. Easing closer, he poked it with the toe of his boot. Whatever was inside was firm and unyielding, rather than soft like garbage.

He sniffed the air, catching the faint scent of decay. Dead animals? Or something worse? Dread cloaked him as he bent to untie the ends of the garbage bag.

The minute the ends fell away, a horrific odor engulfed him. It was all Sam could do not to lose his fried chicken dinner.

He stumbled backward, breathing through his mouth to avoid the awful stench. This was far worse than cow patties, that was for sure.

When he was certain he wouldn't puke, he stepped forward. Donning gloves from his pocket, he gripped the edge of the bag and peered inside.

A man's pale, lifeless face stared up at him.

Not Roy Carlton—it was someone he didn't recognize. The same guy Mari had seen walking the tree line? Maybe. He rummaged for his cell phone and snapped a picture of the dead man's face in case he didn't have an ID on him.

Without disturbing the body, he tried to ascertain how the guy had died. Using a gloved hand, he pushed the corpse to see better. There it was. A bloody mess covered the guy's chest and abdomen, even some pock marks in his face now that he was looking more closely. This damage had not been done by a rifle or handgun.

This was the work of a shotgun.

Unwilling to destroy evidence, he dropped the edge of the bag and stepped away. Stripping off the gloves, he used his phone to call Jackson.

"We haven't found him," Jackson said in lieu of a greeting. "Hate to admit it, but Carlton is in the wind."

"I found a dead guy stuffed in a large garbage bag on Mari Lynch's property." He paused, then continued, "A masked intruder cut the window of her son's bedroom out and attempted to grab the child. Possibly Carlton, himself. She chased him away, so I've been searching her property. I don't know for sure the dead man is related to Carlton's vanishing act, but we need the state crime lab here, pronto."

"You're positive it's not Carlton?" Jackson's voice held a note of hope. "Sure would help us if it was."

He couldn't help smiling. "I'm sure. It's not him. Like I said, Carlton may have tried to grab his son. Mari Lynch saw a man walking down along her the tree line yesterday evening. I'm no expert, but this guy could have been sitting here since then. We'll need the medical examiner to tell us the approximate time of death."

"Do you think she killed him?" Jackson asked.

"No." Although the image of Mari standing on her front porch holding a shotgun, just like that of the murder weapon, flashed in his mind. Was he wrong about her? It wouldn't be the first time he'd trusted the wrong woman.

If he hadn't been with the Texas Rangers, and had intended her or her son harm, he had no doubt she'd have fired first and asked questions later.

"I can't say for sure," he amended. "She has a 12-gauge shotgun. And I believe this guy died of a close encounter with a similar weapon. Forensics will tell us more once they get him out of the garbage bag and on the slab."

Jackson whistled. "Sounds to me like she had the means and potential motive to have done the deed."

Difficult to imagine Mari stuffing a man's body into a garbage bag, unless it was her ex. Besides, someone had tried to abduct her son. "I need to talk to her."

"I'll get the medical examiner and crime scene techs there," Jackson said. "Stick around. Tuck,

Marsh and I will be there soon. We'll need you to pinpoint the location of the body."

"Will do. After I speak with Ms. Lynch, I'll come back to stand guard over him."

Jackson was silent for a moment, as if trying to understand why he would even consider breaking protocol. Sam knew his priority was to protect the woman and her son from Roy Carlton.

"Fine," Jackson finally said. "See y'all, soon."

"Thanks." He disconnected the call. He made one last sweep of the area, making sure no one was lurking nearby. If this was the man Mari had seen, then the body hadn't been here more than twenty-four hours. Remaining untouched except, of course, by whoever had killed him and stuck him in there.

And where was Carlton? He turned and hustled up to the ranch house, hoping he wasn't making a grave mistake.

That Mari Lynch was a victim, not a cold-blooded killer like her ex-husband.

TWO

What was taking him so long? Keeping Theo tucked into a warm blanket on the sofa, Mari had moved from one window to the next, searching for the ranger. He'd spent a fair amount of time in the rear of the house, where the intruder had escaped. Then he'd headed into the woods.

Her father had built the ranch house on the property in a way that the barn out back obstructed her view to a certain extent. It wouldn't have mattered, except for the very real threat of danger.

She silently prayed Roy wasn't lingering nearby. Or maybe it would be better if he was; that way the ranger would find him, arrest him and toss him back in jail.

Where he belonged.

Why had he tried to grab Theo? Questions spun through her mind as she tried to make sense of it all. As far as she could tell, Roy had nothing to gain by coming here. It was, after all, the first place the Rangers had searched for him.

Keeping the shotgun close, she busied herself by making coffee. Normally she didn't drink caffeine this late, but the attempted abduction and Roy's escape from prison convinced her she wouldn't sleep much, anyway.

Not until her ex was no longer a threat.

She wished, not for the first time, that she hadn't married Roy Carlton. Yet she could not regret having Theo. Her son was everything to her. Her main reason for living. She'd named him after her father, Theodore Lynch. And the moment her divorce was final, she'd legally changed their last name back to Lynch.

Glancing at her watch, she wondered again what was taking the deputy so long. A glimpse of movement through the window had her sucking in a harsh breath. Then she relaxed, recognizing Ranger Sam Hayward. His grim facial expression appeared to be carved in stone. He was alone, so she assumed he hadn't found Roy. Yet there was a somber aura about him that indicated something was wrong. Her stomach knotted as she let him in.

"Ma'am." He nodded and removed his hat, running his fingers through his thick dark hair.

"Did you find Roy?" She couldn't help but ask.

"Afraid not."

She bit her lip and turned away. "Help yourself

to some coffee. I need you to watch over Theo while I board up the window in his room."

"Wait." His sharp tone had her turning to face him. "Please sit."

Eyeing him warily, she did so. "What's wrong?" She couldn't take the heavy silence. "You look upset or angry."

He met her gaze. "I found a dead man stuffed in a plastic garbage bag down at Whistling Creek."

What? She blinked, swayed and had to grab the edge of the table to keep from tumbling off the seat. "Roy?"

"Not your ex-husband." He continued holding her gaze, as if he might be able to read her mind. "Possibly the man you'd glimpsed walking along the trees. I'd like you to identify him."

Not Roy. She told herself it was wrong to have hoped Roy would be dead, where he could no longer hurt her or Theo. Then again, it wouldn't make sense that Roy was dead when he'd just tried to grab her son. "I don't understand. Why would someone kill him and leave him on my property?"

"Good question." Sam's gaze slid to her shotgun propped against the wall, then back to her. "Did you shoot him?"

The question was a punch to her chest. For a

moment she couldn't speak, could barely think. Why would he assume she'd killed him?

The shotgun.

"Dear Lord Jesus help me," she whispered in a heartfelt prayer. This couldn't be happening. The man he'd discovered must have been killed with a shotgun.

She found the strength to look at the ranger. "I did not shoot him. Or anyone. I—I couldn't even bring myself to shoot the intruder in the back as he ran away from the house after trying to grab Theo."

His gaze didn't waver from hers. "Maybe this guy threatened you and your son. So you followed him down to the creek and shot him. Your guilt over that act prevented you from being able to shoot the masked intruder."

"I didn't!" There was no way to hide the desperation in her tone. "I wouldn't shoot someone for being on my property."

"Not even Roy Carlton?"

"No." She lowered he gaze. If Roy had come toward her in a threatening manner or had a gun, she may have been able to shoot him. In truth, she'd rather not find out what she was capable of.

Ranger Sam pulled out his phone and thumbed the screen. Then he turned it toward her. "Does he look familiar?"

She inwardly recoiled from the gruesome

sight but forced herself to look at him. Was he a friend of Roy's? Maybe. She searched her memory. "No."

"He's not the guy you saw yesterday?"

She shook her head helplessly. "He was too far away to get a good look at his face. And he walked away from the house, so no. I cannot say that this is the same man."

Wordlessly, he tucked the phone back into his pocket. "I have the medical examiner, crime scene techs and a couple of rangers on the way. I need to head back down to the creek. Please stay inside. We may have more questions for you."

The reality of the situation sank deep into her bones. This was just the beginning. "I called the sheriff's department about the attempt on Theo." She glanced toward the window overlooking her driveway. "I expect Deputy Strawn any minute."

"Good. Hold off on repairing the window until he gets here."

Swallowing hard, she nodded. "Okay. I—do you need to take the shotgun?"

He arched a brow. "Not yet. Shotguns shells are full of pellets as I'm sure you know. It's not like we can match the pellets in this guy's body to the ones in your shotgun shells, the way we can match a slug to the corresponding weapon that fired it."

The fact that he'd already considered it was almost as awful as the way he'd asked her if she'd killed a man.

Then again, she had stepped out to greet him with the barrel of her shotgun. Her nerves were on edge from the recent attempt to grab Theo, but in hindsight, she should have handled his arrival differently.

She inwardly winced at her foolishness.

Without saying anything more, Sam Hayward turned and left. She didn't move as he closed the door behind him.

Who had killed that man and why? Was it connected to Roy's escape? If the dead man was the same guy she'd seen walking past her home, the timing of his death had to be prior to Roy's escape. Yet she felt certain Roy had been here, cutting through the glass of Theo's window and crawling inside to grab him. There's no one else who would want to take her son.

The two incidents had to be connected. But she couldn't begin to comprehend how. Or why.

"Mommy?" She glanced up to see Theo sitting up on the sofa, rubbing his eyes. He wore superhero footie pajamas that were already getting small for him. Her son was growing like a weed. "Is it morning?"

"No, sweetheart. It's late." She stood on shaky legs and crossed to her son. She sat on the sofa, lifted him into her arms and hugged him close. "You should try to get some sleep."

"Did the ranger find the scary man?" Theo asked.

Her heart squeezed at his words. "The ranger, Mr. Sam, has made sure the scary man is long gone. You don't have to worry about him anymore." That wasn't entirely true, but she didn't want her son to be afraid. She was worried sick enough for the both of them.

"I'm thirsty." Theo rested his head on her shoulder. "Can I have chocolate milk?"

She usually saved that treat for special occasions. Tonight she'd make an exception. She forced a smile. "Sure. But then you need to stretch out on the sofa again, okay? We'll pretend we're camping and sleep in the living room tonight."

"Okay."

After setting Theo on his booster seat, she turned to the fridge. She poured a small amount of chocolate milk in a plastic cup and handed it to Theo.

With a grin he took a large gulp. Then he glanced up at the curtain rod over the sink, where she'd recently set the stuffed elf that had been handed down by her father. "Billy the elf is watching me," Theo whispered.

Many of the kids at Theo's preschool shared

antics of their Elf on the Shelf. Harmless fun that helped to keep Theo in line during the Christmas holiday. Since his birthday wasn't too far off, she'd kept the elf theme going even though Christmas had passed.

"He's always watching to see if you're good or bad," she reminded him. "Don't forget, your birthday is coming up. That means you need to listen to me, without complaining."

Theo nodded, his eyes wide. Then he downed the rest of his chocolate milk. Over his shoulder she could see headlights approaching in the distance. Finally Deputy Strawn had arrived.

She lifted her son up and out of his booster seat and carried him to the sofa. He was getting big now that he was almost five. Soon she wouldn't be able to carry him around.

After tucking him in next to Charlie, his stuffed dog, she bent to kiss his cheek. "More policemen are here. Be good and stay here, okay?"

"'Kay." Theo yawned and hugged Charlie close.

She stared down at him for a long moment before heading to the door to let the deputy in.

First Roy or some other masked stranger had tried to abduct Theo and now there was a dead man down by the creek.

What next? She was afraid to find out.

She closed her eyes and lifted her heart in prayer.

Lord Jesus, keep my son safe in Your loving arms. Amen.

Sam was glad to find the dead man's body in the exact same position as when he'd left it. He stayed back, partially because of the smell and to avoid trampling the crime scene any more than he had.

As he gazed around the area, he didn't see any obvious signs of blood. Granted, there could be some farther away, he hadn't checked every inch of the terrain, but the more he considered the location of the garbage bag, the more he believed the guy had been dumped here after being killed elsewhere.

Now that he was here, he knew it wasn't likely Mari Lynch had anything to do with this dead guy. She couldn't have killed him, stuffed him in the bag and dragged him all the way down here. There had been no sign of something heavy being dragged across the hard ground, and he couldn't believe she would do something like this so close to her young son.

But it was entirely possible someone had killed the guy and plopped him here, hoping to implicate her.

And how did this fit into the abduction attempt on her son? Did Mari know something she shouldn't? Was she more involved in Roy's criminal past than she was letting on?

His mind didn't want to go there, but he also knew better than to his trust her. Once burned, twice shy and all that. Besides, she'd handled the shotgun like a pro. Despite her claim that she hadn't been able to shoot at the man running away, he doubted she'd hesitate to protect herself and her son.

His phone vibrated. Pulling it from his pocket, he saw Jackson's name. He didn't even get a chance to say hello.

"Sam? Where are you?"

"Are you in the driveway?" He turned to glance up toward the house. It was far away, but he thought he could see the faint glow of head-lights.

"Yeah, we just pulled in behind a Deputy Strawn. He's interviewing Carlton's ex about the attempted kidnapping. Where is this creek you mentioned?"

Sam gave him directions on how to find the wooded area near Whistling Creek. It didn't take long for Jackson, Marshall and Tucker to hoof it down the property line to join him.

Tuck shook his head when he saw the plastic bag. "Dude must be pretty small to be shoved in there."

"That was my thought, too." Sam stared at the garbage bag. "He's crammed in tight, so I couldn't get a good look."

"You reckon he's missing body parts?" Jackson asked.

Nothing would surprise him at this point. He shrugged. "Anything is possible. I didn't want to disturb the body, so all I did was make sure he was dead."

"I'll take your word for it," Marshall muttered. He tugged the brim of his hat down. "Wonder how long this guy would have been sitting out here if you hadn't come out to check on the ex-wife."

Jackson arched a brow. "Did Carlton's ex-wife send you down here?"

"No, I volunteered to search the area for Roy." He tried not to sound defensive. "A man wearing a ski mask cut through the window of her son's room and tried to grab him."

"So she says," Marshall drawled.

He sighed. "I highly doubt she cut the window herself in the dead of winter. And I'm sure if we talk to the boy, he'll confirm the incident."

There was a moment of silence as the rest of the rangers digested this information.

"Don't like this." Tuck frowned, glancing around the remote area. "Smells like a trap."

"Maybe it was, and our dead guy walked right

into it. Ms. Lynch saw a man headed this way yesterday evening, but she couldn't recognize the picture I took of our guy. Could be she saw him going to meet someone else. Two people came here to discuss something important. One left, the other's dead."

"And they used her property for the meeting place, because—why?" Jackson asked.

"That's a good question. Along with how this dude factors into the abduction attempt on her son." Sam waved a hand. "No blood in the immediate area. First step would be to find the spot where the shooting took place."

"You'd think the ex-wife would have heard a gunshot, even one originating down here," Tucker mused.

Tuck made a good point. "True." He mentally kicked himself for not asking her about that.

Jackson's phone buzzed. "This is the medical examiner." He stepped away to take the call. Sam listened as Jackson provided directions for the rest of the team. The local cops would want in on this, too. But if the dead guy was connected to Roy Carlton, the rangers could pull rank. The Texas Rangers operated under the department of public safety. They handled major crimes, assisted in capturing escaped convicts, investigated public corruption, reviewed cold cases, and just about anything else the governor assigned to them. They only had jurisdiction in Texas, unlike the Federal Marshals who could go across state lines.

Texas was big enough to keep them plenty busy.

Within twenty minutes, the scene around the dead body was lit up brighter than Mari's Christmas tree. The medical examiner stood beside Sam as the crime scene techs photographed the bag, the ground and anything else that seemed remotely interesting.

When the techs and local deputies had spread out to search the surrounding area for the actual crime scene, the medical examiner, an older man with white hair by the name of Earl Bond, stepped up to the body bag. Covered from head to toe in gloves and protective gear, he peeled away the plastic bag, revealing their victim.

The man was bigger than he'd assumed as Earl unfolded him from the confines of the bag. Thankfully, he wasn't missing any body parts. Sam realized the guy had been stuffed in there like a rag doll, easier to do before rigor set in.

When Earl had their victim stretched out on the ground, though, Sam figured his original conjecture about the man's size had been correct. By his estimation, the guy was roughly about five feet eight or nine inches tall. On the shorter side and skinny, too, which had allowed the perp to stuff him in the garbage bag.

"Shotgun blast to the chest," Earl said in a voice muffled by his mask. The smell was worse now that the body was out of the garbage bag and stretched out on the ground. "Based on the amount of decomp, which is slower than normal in cold weather, I'd say he's been here about twenty-four hours give or take a few. I don't see any other wounds, but this light isn't great. I'll know more when I get him on the table."

"No spent shells inside the bag?" Tucker asked.

"Nothing but the victim and body fluids." Earl glanced up at them. "That suggests he was stuffed inside shortly after his death. Maybe even standing in the bag prior to getting shot."

That was an unusual way to kill someone, but the attempt may have been to minimize the mess. Of course, if that was the killer's goal, using a shotgun was counterintuitive. A bullet to the brain would have done the trick.

"Anything else strike you as unusual?" Sam asked.

Earl shrugged. "No ID or wallet, but that's typical. I need to examine him closer. You'll want fingerprints, I assume."

"Yep." Sam gestured for a tech to come over. "Please get his prints so we can run them through AFIS. The sooner we know who he is, the better."

"Okay." The tech went to work. Sam stared at

the dead man's face, wishing he looked even remotely familiar.

"We need to interview Ms. Lynch," Jackson
said. "This is her property, she owns a gun similar to the murder weapon, and if this guy is related to Carlton's escape, we could be looking
at motive."

"I can take the lead." The offer popped out of
Sam's mouth before he could think twice.

Tuck arched a brow. "Oh yeah?"

"I have a rapport with her." Sam needed to
prove to himself, and to his buddies, that he could
be objective. "I think she'll open up to me. Besides, let's not forget someone tried to grab her
son. There's far more to this situation than meets
the eye."

"I'll go with you," Jackson said quickly. "Tuck
and Marshall can stay here."

"Sure, stick us with the dead guy," Tucker muttered sourly.

Sam smiled and clapped him on the shoulder.
"Look on the bright side, he can't talk back."

Turning away, he led the way up to the ranch
house. The light was still on in the kitchen. He
had no doubt Mari Lynch was still awake.

As they stepped up onto the porch the door
opened. To his surprise, she held a hammer in
her hand. He eyed it warily as she stepped back.
"Come in."

"Thanks." He cleared his throat and stepped over the threshold. "This is Ranger Jackson Woodlow. Jackson, this is Ms. Maribelle Lynch."

"Nice to meet you," Mari said. She set the hammer on the table. "Please call me Mari. I—uh, just finished boarding up the window in Theo's room. Would you like coffee?"

"Yes, please," Jackson said.

"Thanks, we'd appreciate that," Sam added.

She filled two mugs and brought them to the table. After a quick glance toward the sofa, where her son was resting, she took a seat. "Did you find Roy? Or get an ID for the dead man?"

"Not yet." He shrugged out of his jacket, then dropped into the chair across from hers. Jackson did the same. "Trust me, finding Roy is important. But we also need to know where you were yesterday."

"All day?" She frowned, tucking a strand of her dark, wavy hair behind her ear. "I start my day gathering eggs from the chicken coop."

"And that's what you did yesterday?" he pressed.

She flushed. "Yes. I fed the chickens then gathered eggs. Then I headed out to check the cattle, making sure they have enough hay to eat and water to drink, and that there weren't any other issues. I make them move around to get their blood circulating when it's cold. When those chores were finished, I took Theo to run errands with me. He's usually in preschool but they're closed between the Christmas and New Year holiday. He's in a 4-K program even though he'll be five on January second. He won't start kindergarten until next year."

"Then what?" Jackson asked. "You had Theo with you the entire time?"

"Yes. I had gathered enough eggs to sell them at the local feedstore. I dropped off four dozen from the past week then picked up a few items at the store for dinner." She folded her hands around her coffee cup. "I came home, checked on the cattle again, gathered more eggs then made lunch. Theo and I played games in the afternoon until dinnertime." She abruptly sighed. "My life is boring. Routine. I take care of the ranch, and my son."

"Please go on," Sam encouraged. "What happened after dinner?"

"I gave Theo an hour of television time while I made another run through the chicken coop for eggs then washed dishes. I was just finishing that when I saw the stranger in the cowboy hat walking near the tree line. I didn't see his face, though. Mostly his back."

"Did you hear gunfire?" Sam asked.

She frowned. "I sometimes hear gunfire in the distance. Mr. Fleming, the rancher next door,

shoots at coyotes who get too close to his livestock. I—honestly may not have paid much attention. But what does any of this have to do
with Roy? He must be the one who tried to abduct Theo."

Before he could answer, a text came in on his
phone. The local police had arrived, and they
knew the dead guy. He lifted his gaze to Mari's.
"Do you know a man by the name of Jeff Abbott?"

The color drained from her face. She stared
at him for a long moment. "I—uh, haven't seen
him in a long time."

"You do know him." He made it a statement,
not a question.

"I—yes. He was the best man at our wedding."

"But you didn't recognize his face when I
showed it to you."

She bit her lip, looking pale. "I—didn't. Maybe
I should have, but I didn't."

It was the connection they needed to Roy Carlton's escape. And maybe even to the recent attempt to snatch Theo.

Unfortunately, it would have been impossible
for Carlton to escape the hospital and to get here
in time to kill his former best man. But he may
have gotten here in time to break into his son's
room.

"Did you get along with Mr. Abbott?" Jackson asked.

Mari spread her hands wide. "I barely knew him. He was at our wedding, but I didn't talk to him much. We didn't hang out together, if that's what you're asking. I doubt I said ten words to him. And that was almost six years ago."

"You don't have any reason to want him dead," Sam said.

A wounded expression darkened her gaze, before she lifted her chin. "No. I haven't seen Jeff since our wedding. And since I was separated for more than a year before I got divorced two years ago, I would have no reason to interact with him." She glared at him. "You still haven't said anything about the attempt to kidnap my son. I'm sorry about Jeff, truly. But you must understand that Theo's safety is my only concern."

"I do, yes," Sam said with a nod. "But I didn't find Roy Carlton nearby."

"Then go out there and keep looking!" She jumped to her feet, pointing to the door, anger darkening her green eyes. "Find him before he tries again."

Sam glanced at Jackson, who gave a slight shrug.

She was right. A dead man shouldn't take priority over a near kidnapping. And the two incidents were obviously related. "We will."

"Ma'am," Jackson said with a nod.

As they left, he glanced over his shoulder to

see her standing there, her arms crossed over her chest, looking as if she were on the brink of falling apart.

And it made him angry with himself that he wanted to go back inside to comfort her.

THREE

Mari held it together long enough to shut the door behind the two men. After clicking the dead bolt into place, she sank into a chair and buried her face in her hands.

What in the world was going on? Where was Roy? Why had he come to take Theo? And who had killed Jeff Abbott with a shotgun, leaving him on her property?

To frame her? Possibly, but she hadn't been arrested.

At least, not yet.

Even that didn't make a lot of sense. What was the point of sending her to jail? She was hardly rich, barely managing to keep the ranch turning a profit. Sure, the two hundred and fifty acres of land, the modest home and outbuildings, including the original ranch house, were worth roughly six million on paper. But in truth there were lots of ranches for sale in the state of Texas, and precious few buyers willing to sign on the dotted line for long hours of work with little profit to show for it. "Land rich, cash poor" was how ranchers saw themselves.

Taking several deep breaths, she pulled herself together. She had not murdered anyone. Had she heard a gunshot sometime last night? She searched her memory but couldn't say for certain. And she would have been concerned about a gunshot after seeing a stranger. Maybe she'd been asleep. Yet living alone with Theo made her more likely to awaken easily.

She swallowed hard. Not hearing or reporting the gunfire wouldn't help prove her innocence. It wasn't easy, but she would place her trust in the process. Put her faith in the Texas Rangers' ability to find Roy and the truth about who had killed Jeff Abbott.

The more she thought about it, the more she struggled to understand what her ex hoped to accomplish by grabbing Theo. A ransom? Forcing her hand to what, sign over the ranch? He was an escaped convict on the run, it wasn't as if he could stay here and live his life.

But he could force her to sign the ranch over to someone else.

A chill snaked down her spine. That must be it. How that motive factored into the murder of Jeff Abbott, she had no idea.

She stood and carried the empty coffee mugs

to the sink. Then she headed to the master bedroom to grab another quilt.

Through the window, she could see the glow of lights in the distance. For all she knew, they would be down at the crime scene for hours yet. Would the presence of the lawmen keep Roy at bay?

She prayed it would.

Turning, she headed back to the living room sofa. Theo had fallen asleep, Charlie tucked under his chin. She stretched out beside him, hiking the quilt to her chest.

She tried to relax, but her mind kept jumping from Roy's escape from prison, his attempt to grab Theo and then to Jeff's murder.

It was hard to admit how naive she'd been to marry Roy Carlton. He'd seemed so nice, and attentive. But if she were honest, she could remember a few instances when his temper had flared, his eyes turning ice-cold.

Why she'd ignored the red flags, she couldn't say. She'd just chosen to believe the words he said, rather than his actions. Once they were married, things had changed. First he'd used his tongue to lash out, but his anger had escalated to him slapping her. Then one night, he'd smacked her hard enough that she'd fallen to the floor.

Never again.

She opened her eyes and stared up at the ceiling. Then she turned to gaze at the Christmas tree. The twinkling lights didn't bring her joy the way they usually did.

How had Roy escaped? Ranger Sam Hayward had claimed it shouldn't have happened, but she didn't know how Roy had pulled it off.

Unless he'd had help.

Jeff Abbott was dead, so he couldn't have been Roy's accomplice. But someone else must have set the escape plan in motion. Maybe Roy had threatened to expose others if they didn't help him get out of jail.

She wouldn't put anything past him. He was cruel enough to threaten to take her son from her, knowing Theo was the most important person in her life.

Her son was the *only* person in her life.

She must have dozed because she awoke with a start. Shifting the quilt out of the way, she rose and looked outside. Sam Hayward's SUV was gone. As were the police cars. She rushed into her bedroom, and discovered the area down by the creek was dark. A shiver slid down her spine as she realized the police and rangers were gone.

She was alone with Theo.

A wave of apprehension washed over her. Had they given up searching for Roy? There was a part of her that was glad Jeff's dead body had been taken away. But the acres of ranchland stretched endlessly around her. The Whistling Creek Ranch was closer to Austin than San Antonio. Her property was relatively remote, with plenty of trees and scrub brush that might provide places for Roy—or anyone else for that matter—to hide.

Jeff's dead body was proof of that.

She turned away from the window and returned to the living room. The police and rangers had searched the area, making sure Roy wasn't nearby. After all, finding her escaped ex was the only reason Sam Hayward had come.

To find Roy. And to let her know about his escape.

Yet she couldn't sit still. She'd nailed plywood over Theo's missing window, but that didn't mean Roy wouldn't try again. Moving from window to window, she was slightly reassured when there was no sign of anyone lurking nearby.

Her father's shotgun was tucked in the corner between the kitchen cabinet and the wall. She took it now and held it beneath her arm, the muzzle pointing to the floor.

She didn't like having a gun around the house, especially with her almost-five-year-old living there. She'd taught Theo to stay away from the weapon, and he'd been good about that so far. But she would feel much better once Roy was tossed back in jail and the man who'd murdered Jeff was caught.

Soon, Lord, please? I ask You to provide guid-

ance for the police to find those responsible. And please, keep Theo safe in Your care!

The prayer brought a bit of comfort to her ragged nerves. Since the hour was approaching four in the morning, she decided to give up on sleep. This was going to be one of those days where she drank an inordinate amount of coffee.

The Christmas lights along the front of the house, combined with the Christmas tree in the corner of the living room, provided enough illumination that she didn't need to turn on additional lighting. Once the coffee was ready, she carried the mug into the living room, propped the shotgun within reach, then sank into the cushy rocker recliner that had once been her dad's favorite.

Oh, how she missed him, especially at times like this. Her father had dedicated his life to ranching, taking over the land from his father, her grandfather. Her mother had passed away when she was twenty years old and away at college. Maybe that loss had played a role in her falling for Roy.

Or maybe he'd exploited her feelings and manipulated her, by being the kind and supportive boyfriend she'd needed.

Only to let his real personality leak through once they were married. She'd been on the brink of leaving him when she'd discovered she was pregnant.

She sincerely tried to make things work. But it was only a year after Theo was born that Roy first slapped her. The second blow was harder. She'd finally confided in her father and had returned home to the ranch. Two weeks later, Roy was arrested for murder. She'd filed for divorce that same day, regardless of the outcome of his trial. Yet it had still taken a full year for her divorce to become final.

Secretly, she'd been relieved to use it as an excuse to cut him from her and Theo's life. Thankfully, the judge had agreed to grant her sole custody of their son.

It had been no surprise that Roy had been found guilty. And that should have been the end of the terror.

Clearly, it wasn't.

Losing her father fourteen months ago had felt as if God had pulled the rug out from underneath her. She'd leaned on her faith, but it wasn't easy. Obviously, she knew what ranching entailed, having grown up doing chores. It made her smile that her dad had chosen to use four-wheelers rather than horses to ride the property. But being the sole owner and operator of the ranch was a huge responsibility.

She desperately needed to keep the ranch profitable, not just for herself, but for Theo.

Would her son even want the legacy of the

ranch? She told herself this wasn't the time to worry about that. Her only goal was to provide a safe and happy childhood for him.

It didn't seem like too much to ask.

"Mommy?"

She turned to see Theo sitting up on the sofa again. She quickly moved over to join him. He burrowed against her, his face turned so he could see the Christmas tree lights.

"Is it time to get up?"

"Not yet, it's still the middle of the night." Normally, he slept until seven.

There was nothing normal about this night.

"Did the police catch the scary man?"

She closed her eyes and wished desperately the answer was yes. "Not yet, but soon. We're safe here. No one will hurt us."

He nodded, relaxing against her, seemingly mesmerized by the lights on the tree. Holding him close, she pressed a kiss to the top of his head, enjoying the scent of his baby shampoo.

This was a keen reminder of how God had blessed her. This was worth facing adversity.

And she silently promised once again to do whatever was necessary to protect her son.

Hiding in a thatch of brush that provided him a direct visual of Mari's ranch house, Sam stamped his feet to increase circulation to his lower extremities. Man, it was cold. He breathed on his gloved hands, attempting to infuse them with warmth.

Allowing his fingers and toes to go numb would not help if he had to act quickly to apprehend Roy Carlton.

Or the perp who had murdered Jeff Abbott.

Tucker, Marshall and Jackson had eyed him suspiciously when he'd offered to stand guard near the Whistling Creek Ranch in case either Roy or the killer showed up. But they hadn't argued, simply letting him know to call if he needed anything.

Yeah, the only thing he needed was a bonfire or a space heater. The way things were going, he'd turn into an ice sculpture before morning.

He couldn't stand the idea of Roy returning to make a second attempt to grab the boy. And no matter how comfortable Mari was with a shotgun, he didn't consider her a suspect either.

The abduction attempt on her son was enough to convince him she was an innocent victim in this. Jackson thought it was suspicious that she hadn't recognized the dead man. Sam figured the guy had been nothing more than a blip on her radar.

He was touched by the loving and caring way she treated her son. His own mother had abandoned him when he was eight. His father had moved in with his parents so they could help raise him. He'd never seen or heard from his mother again.

After joining the Texas Rangers, he'd searched for her. It wasn't hard. He'd discovered she'd died of a drug overdose four years after she'd left him. In hindsight, her leaving him with his father to be raised with his grandparents was probably the best thing she could have done. Yet he still hated knowing she hadn't cared enough to enter rehab and get clean.

Old news, he thought. Not important tonight. Yeah, the longer he stood there, the more he realized it had been foolish to stand guard like this. The likelihood of Roy returning here so soon was slim.

But he couldn't turn his back on a single mother and her son, knowing they were in potential danger.

He decided to take another walk around the property to keep his blood moving. He'd made the loop around the ranch house, barn and main pasture twice now, without seeing anything suspicious. The last time he'd gone past, the cattle hadn't even bothered to look at him.

His breath came out in puffs as he crossed the yard, dead grass, leaves and sticks crunching beneath his feet. He would have given just about anything for a cup of hot coffee, but that would have to wait.

Safety first. Creature comforts came second.

A spike of adrenaline helped warm him from the inside out. Every sense on alert, he moved slowly and carefully, making his way down the property line. It was the same path he'd taken earlier that night. The one leading to Whistling Creek.

And Jeff Abbott's dead body.

While the crime scene techs had worked on collecting evidence, including discovering the location of a bloody area roughly fifty yards farther back from the location of the body near the creek, where they believed the actual crime had taken place—he and the others had learned that Jeff Abbott was the stepson of Grayson Beaumont, the mayor of Austin, Texas.

Which was very interesting, since Roy had been convicted of murdering the mayor's city manager, Hank George. Word on the street was that Mayor Grayson Beaumont and City Manager Hank George had been close. So why kill Jeff Abbott, the mayor's stepson? Was this related to Hank George's murder? Was someone sending a message to the mayor by killing those close to him? Or was this related to something else?

Something illegal? In his mind, that was the working theory.

That political link had sealed the deal of the case remaining with the Texas Rangers. The governor had called their chief personally, who had then called Sam to request he take the lead in the investigation into Hank George's murder and Carlton's subsequent escape.

He would not, could not, mess this up by allowing a pretty face to distract him. One colossal mistake in trusting the wrong woman was enough. He'd been taken in by a pretty face and a sob story about abuse, only to be drawn into a trap that had nearly killed him and his fellow rangers.

Given that, he wasn't about to trust Mari so easily.

Despite being chilled to the bone, he didn't hurry as he encircled the property, carefully scanning his surroundings. He wondered just how much of the acreage Mari owned beyond the pastures and grazing areas that stretched before him.

Using his phone, he'd done a bit of research on her but hadn't learned much. He'd found the obituary related to her father's death, but that was about all.

There had been no sign of her on social media, which had been surprising. Then again, maybe not, considering her ex-husband was a murderer.

He wasn't active on social media, either, but that was due to his being in law enforcement and making more than a few enemies along the course of his career.

He paused at the corner of the barn, accustomed now to the pungent scent and sounds of the animals around him. Seeing nothing alarming, he moved on to the chicken coop, then headed back up around the corner of the house until he was out front.

He abruptly stopped when he caught a glimpse of Mari holding her son on the sofa. The two of them seemed to gaze at the brightly lit Christmas tree tucked in the corner of the room, although from this angle it was hard to say for certain.

His heart squeezed in his chest at the poignant sight.

Mari was beautiful with her long, dark hair and green eyes. Incredibly amazing in how she so obviously cared for her son.

Tuck was right. His emotions were getting the better of him, and not in a good way.

He eased back, staying out of sight. For one thing, he didn't want to frighten her. For another, he wasn't there to spy on her like some peeping Tom.

His intent had been honorable. He'd stayed behind to make sure Roy Carlton or some other perp didn't show up to make another grab at Theo. Or worse.

A fear that was apparently unjustified.

He moved back even farther, far enough that he couldn't see inside the house without using a scope.

Still, it wasn't easy to push the image of Mari and Theo from his mind as he continued walking the perimeter. It was tempting to head for the road and walk the half mile until he reached the wooded spot where he'd left his SUV.

Staying here was a mistake. All he'd accomplished was adding to the confusion in his mind over Mari and freezing his backside off.

Bad news all around.

The snap of a twig caught his attention. He froze, then lowered into a crouch while sweeping his gaze around the area.

Wildlife? Or something more threatening?

He was almost seventy yards from the ranch house. He silently moved into a better position so that he could see the front porch, the string of Christmas lights and the large picture window in the living room.

Mari and Theo were still on the sofa. Long seconds passed, without any other sound disturbing the silence of the night. Sam figured the sound had been from either a white-tailed deer or maybe a coyote.

Yet something kept him hiding there. Waiting. Watching.

His gaze narrowed on a small patch of brush

located directly across from the ranch house. Had the branches moved?

He frowned. There was a gentle breeze coming in from the north, but not enough to have made the tree limbs sway.

Tucking his chin, he breathed into the front of his leather jacket. If someone was out there, he didn't want to give away his location with his breath making puffs of steam in the air.

For long minutes all was still. He couldn't see anyone hiding over there, and mentally kicked himself for not bringing a pair of binoculars.

He'd just convinced himself that his mind was playing tricks on him, when he saw movement again. Narrowing his gaze, he held his breath and watched.

His blood coalesced into ice.

There was a man out there. The perp was stretched out on the cold hard ground, which was why he hadn't noticed him.

But there was no mistaking him now. And worse, Sam was pretty sure the guy had a rifle.

Roy Carlton? Or someone else?

With excruciating slowness, he pulled his Sig Sauer P320 from his belt holster. The guy was a good seventy-five yards away and close to the ground, making accuracy with a handgun a challenge.

The distance didn't concern him. Firing a warning shot would be just as effective. He preferred to take the perp alive, especially if the man out there was Carlton.

Too bad there was no decent cover between his current position and the guy. Impossible to sneak up behind him.

So be it. Sam lifted and sighted his weapon, preparing to fire at a spot above the gunman's head.

The sharp crack from the rifle came first, followed by the sound of glass breaking. Less than a nanosecond later, Sam fired in return, even as his heart thudded painfully in his chest.

The shooter had targeted the large picture window, the same location where Mari had been sitting with her son!

Had they been hit? He thumbed 911 on his phone without taking his eyes off the location of the shooter. Just as the dispatcher answered, he saw movement within the brush. A dark shadow rose to his feet.

No! He was going to get away!

Abandoning the call, Sam sprinted after the perp, desperately wishing his fellow rangers were there to back him up.

FOUR

When the window behind her shattered seconds after she heard gunfire, Mari instinctively ducked, then rolled off the sofa and onto the floor with Theo, covering his small body with hers.

Roy was out there!

Theo began to cry; the loud crack of gunfire and the broken window had frightened him. It had scared her, too. She was afraid to stand, worried Roy would take a second shot at them. But they needed to get out of there.

Far away from the ranch house.

"It's okay, Theo. We're fine. We'll get to safety." Striving to remain calm, she waited for one agonizing minute then the next, before lifting herself up on her hands and knees. She raised her head and tried to see over the back of the sofa but couldn't.

She still had the quilt and took a moment to toss it over the broken shards of glass covering the floor. It was the best she could do under the circumstances. "We're going to crawl down the hall, okay? Can you do that?"

Theo sniffled loudly and nodded. "Is the scary man out there?"

A helpless wave of fury hit hard. Why was Roy doing this? Traumatizing his own son? He'd escaped from prison—why hadn't he headed south to cross the Mexican border? Did he honestly hate her this much? She swallowed hard. "I'm not sure what happened. Could be Mr. Fleming is shooting at coyotes again and missed."

"He hit our house?" Theo's eyes were wide.

She didn't want to lie to him, but she didn't want to scare him more than he already was. "I really don't know. We're going to keep our heads down, just in case. We need to crawl down the hall to my room."

Theo nodded and held his stuffed dog in one hand as he crawled with her across the living room and toward the hallway leading to the bedrooms. There was no more gunfire, but she couldn't help but think that Roy was still out there.

Waiting for a second chance to kill them.

Please, Lord Jesus, keep us safe in Your care!

The silent prayer helped soothe her nerves. The most important thing now was that she and Theo were unharmed. Yet they couldn't stay here at the ranch house.

Her car was in the garage and that faced the same direction from where the gunfire had originated. The car would have been better, but thankfully, she had the four-wheelers out back in the barn.

Using one of them should help her get Theo to the Fleming property. She didn't like the idea of placing the older man in harm's way, but what choice did she have?

She would do whatever was necessary to save her son.

Mari paused in the hallway, remembering her phone was still on the kitchen counter. Unfortunately, the shotgun was in the living room. Should she go back to grab it? Maybe not. But the phone was a necessity.

She hesitated, then rose to a crouch just high enough to snatch it off the charger. Then she and Theo continued crawling to the master bedroom as she used her thumb to dial 911. As earlier, she doubted the response would be quick, but she made the call anyway.

"911, what is your emergency," the calm female voice on the other end of the line asked.

"This is Mari Lynch at the Whistling Creek Ranch. Someone shot through the front window of my house. My son and I are in danger. Send the police!"

"Okay, I'm dispatching two deputies to your home right now. Are you or your son hurt?"

Did being scared to death count? Probably not. "We're not hurt. But the shooter could still be outside! I need you to hurry."

"I'm here for you, ma'am. Please stay on the line."

"I can't." She couldn't take care of Theo while holding her phone. "Just get the deputies here as quickly as possible." Without saying anything more, she disconnected and shoved the phone in her pocket. Then she rose to her feet and scooped Theo into her arms.

"This way." She entered her room, staying away from the bedroom windows. It was possible Roy would have already run around to the back of the house. "In the closet."

It was the only place she could think of to use as a safe hideout for Theo.

Her son crawled inside the space, clutching Charlie to his chest. She quickly changed into warm clothing, suitable for heading outside. Her hands were shaking, but she did her best to stay focused.

The goal was to avoid being hit by gunfire while getting Theo out of there safely. No easy task. She was about to head into Theo's room for his clothes when she heard a voice calling her name.

"Mari? It's Sam. Are you and Theo okay?"

Sam? She hesitated. Why would Sam be here? The male voice didn't sound like Roy's, but she hadn't seen him in so long she couldn't be sure it wasn't her ex-husband out there trying to play a trick on her. She pressed her hand to her mouth to keep from screaming.

"Mari? Please tell me you're both okay." The low male voice held a note of urgency. "I saw the guy who shot your window, but he got away."

She bit down hard on her lip, trying to understand what happened. How could Sam have seen the guy who shot at her house?

"Mari?" His voice was louder now, and she finally opened her bedroom door to peer out. Sam hovered in the hallway, concern etched on his features. "I had to crawl through the broken window to get in, as you had the dead bolt on. Where's Theo? Is he okay, too?"

"You were watching my house outside in the cold?" She hadn't meant for her tone to sound accusing.

"Yes. I was worried Roy might come back." He held her gaze. "I'm sorry I wasn't fast enough to prevent him from taking that shot. I fired back, but he took off running. I gave chase but lost him on the road. He had a car stashed there and managed to escape before I could grab him."

"Mommy?" Theo's voice came from the closet.

"Right here, sweetie." She turned toward the open closet door. "You can come out, now. Mr. Sam is here to help us."

Theo came over to stand beside her. He gazed up at Sam. "Did you find the scary man?"

"I chased him away," Sam said. "And I promise to protect you and your mom so you don't have to be afraid of the scary man, okay?"

"Okay." Her son nodded, then turned his face into her side as if suddenly shy. She put her arm around his slim body, hugging him close.

She found herself relaxing just a bit. She eyed Sam critically, noticing how red his face was from the cold. "You must be freezing if you were really outside all this time. I can make coffee."

"Stay here for a few minutes. I want to board up that front window." Sam hesitated, then added, "I called 911. Deputies should be on the way."

"I called them as well. Thanks for taking care of the window."

Sam nodded and moved away.

Having Sam there helped tremendously. It made sense that the Rangers would have someone watching her house in case Roy decided to return.

And he had. Or someone had, she silently amended. To be fair, she didn't know for sure the shooter was Roy. It could be someone Roy had hired.

But why? Getting access to the ranch was the only thing that made sense, but killing her wouldn't help Roy get his hands on it.

However, kidnapping Theo could possibly lead to that. Even so, it didn't quite make sense. Unless Roy's accomplices didn't know the true financial status of the ranch.

"Mommy? I'm hungry." Theo gazed up at her with light blue eyes that he'd inherited from his father.

"Soon. First we need to get you out of your pajamas." She knew there would be no going back to sleep after this. "When Mr. Sam has the window fixed, I'll make breakfast."

Theo nodded and turned to grab his stuffed dog from the closet floor. Without putting up a fuss, he allowed her to take him into his room for clothes. The bedroom was chilly, so they didn't linger.

"Mari? You and Theo can come out now," Sam called.

He'd gotten the window fixed faster than she'd anticipated. She took Theo's hand and led him back to the kitchen. The living area was much darker with the large sheets of plywood covering the window. Sam had picked up the shards of glass, too, and placed the quilt on the sofa. Shivering, she crossed over to feed more wood into the cast-iron, wood-burning stove.

"I'll do that," Sam quickly offered.

"Oh, uh, thanks. I'll start the coffee and then make breakfast." She wasn't used to having someone to pitch in with chores. Taking a moment to snag the shotgun, more to keep it out of Theo's reach, she hurried into the kitchen.

She set the shotgun in the alcove near the pantry, then went to work. Making coffee didn't take long. She had plenty of eggs and some leftover bacon, too.

"Scrambled or over easy?" she asked.

"Whatever you're having is fine." Sam flashed a smile. "I like them either way."

"Theo prefers scrambled, if that's okay."

"Works for me." Sam scowled and crossed to the kitchen window. "I'm surprised the deputies aren't here yet."

"One of the downsides of living out here." She poured coffee into a mug and handed it to him. "Hopefully, they'll arrive soon."

"We may need to relocate you and Theo to a safe house," he said in a low voice. "Just long enough for us to find and arrest Roy Carlton."

She frowned, then turned back to the stove. She turned the bacon, before glancing at him. "I want to be safe and to have Roy arrested as soon as possible. But I can't just leave the livestock to perish. I depend on both the eggs from my chickens and meat from the cattle to provide for us."

"I understand your concern," he agreed. "But if you're staying, then so am I."

She glanced at him over her shoulder. On one hand, he had some nerve announcing he was moving into her home. Then again, Roy had tried to kidnap Theo, and had fired at them through the window.

"Okay. Then we'll stay here together," she said. Sam was far too attractive for her peace of mind, but she trusted him to keep her safe. Theo, too.

She hoped and prayed the rest of the rangers worked twice as hard to find Roy so her life could return to normal.

Sam knew Tuck, Marsh and Jackson would have a fit when they learned he'd offered to stay indefinitely, providing Mari and Theo his protection. It wasn't smart to get emotionally involved, yet he had made the right decision to stay on the property overnight. A gunman had shown up and nearly killed the young mother and her son.

Roy or one of his accomplices? He couldn't say for sure but had called Tucker to let him know about the incident. Unfortunately, the rear plate of the truck was covered in mud, so he hadn't been able to get a plate number. He did give Tuck a general description of the vehicle, though, and had a feeling his fellow rangers would all be here soon enough.

And where in the world were those deputies? A single mother living alone and reporting gunfire should have garnered a quicker response.

Seconds later, he heard the rumble of car engines. He moved toward the closest window and nodded with satisfaction when he noticed two squads had responded.

It was about time. He set his coffee on the table, then moved to the door. "The deputies are here."

"Okay. I'll hold off on making the eggs until we're finished." She handed her son a strip of bacon and a sippy cup she'd filled with chocolate milk. "Behave, Theo. We need to talk to the policemen."

Theo nodded, gulping his milk. The little boy was a trouper, handing all the commotion better than Sam had expected.

It made him angry to know that the little boy and his mother were living in fear. First the attempted kidnapping, then finding Abbott's dead body and now this.

It all had to be related to Roy Carlton. Or his accomplices. He really wished he'd been able to grab the shooter.

The two deputies identified themselves as Adam Grendel and Trey Drake.

Grendel took the lead. "We received two 911 calls about this shooting. From each of you?" He pointed to him and Mari.

"Yes. I'm Texas Ranger Sam Hayward. I'm working with several rangers to find escaped convict Roy Carlton. Ms. Mari Lynch is Roy's ex-wife."

"I heard on the way over that there was also an attempted abduction, earlier?" Grendel asked. "Strawn took that call."

"Yes, a masked man broke into my son Theo's room and tried to take him." Mari put her hands on Theo's shoulders. "I threatened him with my shotgun and he took off."

"A scary man," Theo added.

"I see." Grendel turned to Sam. "And you just happened to be sitting on the property when a gunman fired through the main window?"

"Yes. I stayed because I was afraid Roy Carlton would return to finish what he'd started. And it seems as if he did." Grendel's statement about the window had him abruptly turning and crossing the living room. He ran his fingers over the wall across from the window. "The slug must be here someplace."

The deputies came over to join him. A minute later, he found it. "Here," he said.

Drake got his knife out and cut around the drywall to get to the slug. He made a point of not getting too close to the bullet fragment, so as to preserve it. When he had the area of drywall cut,

Drake removed the entire chunk and place it in a large evidence bag.

"It's a little mangled, but we may get something off this," Drake said.

"Good eye," Grendel said grudgingly. "Do you have any other evidence?"

"I'm afraid not. I saw the shooter stretched out on the ground beneath a tree. I was about to fire over his head to get his attention when he shot the window. I fired back and he jumped up from the ground and took off running. I chased after him, but he had a vehicle stashed down the road. The rear plate was covered in mud. I only have a make and model—a Chevy truck with a covered bed. Dark in color."

He didn't add that he'd already given the same information to Tucker Powell. It wasn't that he didn't trust the sheriff's deputies to do their job, but they weren't as invested in the Roy Carlton case as he and the other rangers were.

"Tell me about the attempted abduction," Grendel said.

Mari explained the incident. When she mentioned that Sam had arrived before the deputy Grendel gave him a narrow look. It was almost as if Grendel suspected he was responsible.

"I came to let Ms. Lynch know that her ex-husband had escaped," he explained. "I was glad to be here so quickly to help search for him. And that's when I found the dead body of Jeff Abbott."

Grendel stared at him, then muttered something under his breath. "Why did you call us if this is a Rangers case?"

He was starting to wonder the same thing. "Look, I think it's important to have these attempts on record. We believe they're related to Roy Carlton's escape but don't know that for sure. There could be something else going on here that we're not aware of."

His phone buzzed from a text. It was from Tuck, announcing he and the others were ten minutes out.

He texted back a quick okay sign, glad to know they'd be there soon.

"Okay, we'll look into this," Grendel said. "And I would appreciate if you would keep us informed on what you find out, too, Hayward. This ranch is within our jurisdiction."

"Of course." Sam didn't hesitate to agree but knew that passing key information on to the deputies wouldn't be at the top of his list. "Thanks for coming out to take the report."

"You need to show us that tree where you saw the shooter," Grendel said.

"Okay." He shrugged into his sheepskin coat and settled his cowboy hat on his head. "Let's go."

He followed Grendel and Drake outside, closing the front door securely behind him.

"You really think this is all related to her ex-husband escaping from jail?" Drake asked.

"Yeah, I do." Sam led them to the tree. The three of them crouched around the area and played their flashlights over the trampled ground. Sam hadn't taken the time to inspect the ground, deciding to head inside to make sure Mari and Theo weren't okay instead.

Now he saw the shell casing the shooter had left behind. Drake carefully placed it in another evidence bag. "We'll get this checked for prints."

"Thanks." Sam rose to his feet. He doubted the shooter had left his prints, but anything was possible. And it was a good find. They had a shell casing and a mangled slug. Both could help narrow down a potential shooter.

The two deputies spent a few more minutes looking around, then headed to their respective squads. Sam jogged back up to the house.

"Did they leave?" Mari glanced over her shoulder, looking at him in surprise. She was making scrambled eggs for Theo and the domestic scene reminded him of Saturday mornings with his grandmother.

"Yeah. But the good news is they found a shell casing. It doesn't sound like much, but the evidence will help when we find him."

"I hope you're right." Her gaze was troubled. "Are you ready to eat?"

"I—uh, sure." He shrugged out of his coat and hung up his hat. "I should warn you that the other rangers I'm working with on this will be here soon."

She lifted her brow. "I'll make more bacon."

"You're not obligated to feed us," he protested. Even as his stomach rumbled loudly.

"Sounds like I do." She managed a smile. "Truly, it's no bother. I'd rather keep busy."

He could understand that. One of the reasons he liked working in law enforcement was that it was never boring. He picked up his coffee mug. "Do you mind if I have a little more?"

"Please help yourself."

Moving toward the pot, he caught a whiff of her flowery scent. Why was he so attracted to her? It wasn't as if he hadn't seen beautiful women before, because he had.

Having made mistakes in the past, he wasn't too anxious to repeat them. He gave himself a stern, silent lecture to stay focused. He was here to find Roy Carlton, uncover who'd tried to kidnap Theo and why, and who'd murdered Jeff Abbott.

Nothing more.

When Mari finished with the scrambled eggs, she filled two plates, setting one in front of him.

She took a seat beside Theo, and then looked at him. "I would like to say grace."

"Ah, okay." The first thing that popped into his mind was that his grandmother would have loved Mari. Then he lowered his head and clasped his hands together.

"Dear Lord, we thank You for this food we are about to eat. We ask that You continue to keep us all safe in Your care. Amen."

"Amen." He lifted his gaze. "I haven't prayed in a long time."

She tipped her head to the side. "God is still there, waiting for you."

He nodded and dug into his meal. He couldn't help but wonder if God had sent him here last night and kept him here throughout the early morning hours.

If anyone deserved to be in God's protection, it was Mari and her son, Theo.

And he added a silent prayer that he and the other rangers would be granted the strength and wisdom they needed to keep them safe.

FIVE

She ate her scrambled eggs and bacon even though she wasn't hungry. Only because she would need her strength to get through this.

Having Sam staying in the ranch house made Mari feel safe. A feeling she would never again take for granted. After the abduction attempt of her son, followed by the gunfire shattering the front window, she wondered if they'd ever be safe again without Sam being there.

They ate in silence for a few minutes until Theo began to fuss. "I want to get down."

She hesitated, glancing at Sam. Was it safe for Theo to run around the house the way he usually did? At almost five years old, her son had an abundance of energy.

"He should stay in the living room and kitchen area," Sam advised. "My fellow rangers should be here soon. They'll help do another search of the property to make sure the—uh—" He hesitated, obviously not wanting to say too much in front of her son. "That the area is clear," he amended.

"Okay." She rose and crossed to the sink to get a dishrag. After wiping Theo's hands and face, she pulled his chair back so he could climb down from the booster seat. "You heard Mr. Sam. You need to stay here in the living room where we can see you."

"What about my horses? And my tractors?" Theo pouted.

She glanced at her half-eaten breakfast. She was about to go to his room to grab his favorite toys when Sam spoke.

"Theo, please wait in the living room until your mother is finished eating."

Her son glanced at him warily. The only real father figure in Theo's life had been her father, whom he called Pop Pop.

Then to her surprise, Theo nodded and went into the living room, scooping up his stuffed dog.

"Thanks." She resumed her seat.

"I didn't mean to interfere with your parenting," Sam said in a low voice. "But I was hoping to give you a few more minutes of peace to enjoy your meal."

She simply nodded and dug into her eggs, which were already lukewarm. "It's not always easy being a single parent. Theo is a good boy most of the time, but he sometime pushes the limits." She managed a half smile. "I will be both happy and sad when he starts full-time kindergarten in the fall."

"I can imagine." She noticed Sam's gaze followed her son as he played with Charlie, having his stuffed dog jump from one sofa cushion to the next. "I want you to know I'll do whatever is necessary to protect you and Theo."

The sweet promise made tears prick her eyes. It had been a long time since anyone had cared about her. And Sam's kindness only reinforced how awful Roy had been.

Not that she needed any reminders about what her ex was capable of after what she'd experienced over the past twelve hours.

"I really don't understand why Roy would kidnap Theo." She finished her eggs and bacon, pushing her plate away. "It doesn't make sense. I don't have money to pay any sort of ransom."

Sam's gaze was curious. "What about selling off some of the land? Wouldn't that bring in some extra cash?"

She shrugged. "If there's a willing buyer, sure. But we're far enough from Austin and San Antonio that commuting back and forth to work wouldn't be easy. There's also a new housing development going up just outside of Austin, too. I wouldn't get top dollar for anything I sold off, and that probably wouldn't be enough of a motive to kidnap a small boy."

"Maybe Carlton is desperate," he suggested.

She cradled her coffee mug in her hands, eyeing him over the rim. "You're the one who told me he had help escaping from the hospital. Wouldn't those same helpers give him cash to disappear across the border into Mexico? I just can't fathom why he'd come here to the first place you and the other rangers would search for him."

"I agree his thought process doesn't make any sense." Sam stood and carried his dirty dishes to the sink. She rose to do the same. Then turned to find Theo standing beside her.

"You said I could play with my toys." His whiny tone grated on her nerves. Then she felt bad, knowing it was just her own lack of sleep making her crabby.

"Sure. Stay here, okay? I'll get them." She gave Sam a quick glance, thankful when he smiled and nodded. Then she hurried down the hall to Theo's bedroom and filled her arms with as many of his favorites as she could, then lugged them to the living room.

She put them on the floor near the Christmas tree. Theo dropped on the floor beside her and grabbed the tall horses, his favorites.

"Giddy up!" He was at that age where he loved cowboys, horses and action figures. She hoped he liked the cowboy action figures she'd purchased for his birthday.

Rising to her feet, she abruptly stopped when she saw Sam peering out the door. "What is it?"

"Nothing to worry about," he said with a smile. "The guys are here."

"Oh, sure. Bring them inside. I'll make them breakfast, too."

"Wait until we check the area. That comes first." He opened the door and stepped outside onto the porch. A few minutes later, he returned with the three additional Texas Rangers.

"Mari, I'm sure you remember Tucker, Marshall and Jackson." He gestured to each man in order.

"Yes, of course." She dried her hand on a dish towel, offering a smile. "Thanks for coming."

"We want to find this guy," Tucker said, frowning at the plywood over the window. "We were wondering if you could draw a map of the property."

"Absolutely." That was a good idea. She went to Theo's room to get his large drawing book and water-soluble markers, then returned to the kitchen. She hesitated, imagining the property, and began to draw.

She started with the house, the barn, the paddock where the cattle were kept in the winter.

"How many acres total?" Sam asked.

"Two hundred and fifty." She glanced up. "I know that sounds like a lot, but just remember that property in general is only worth what someone is willing to pay."

"What's that?" Tucker asked, leaning over her other shoulder and tapping to a square she'd drawn on the map not far from Whistling Creek.

"There's a small ranch house back there that was originally built by my grandfather. We use it sometimes as quarters for ranch hands helping in the summer. It's rustic, but I do have propane gas, water and electric out there."

The rangers looked at each other. "Does Roy know about it?"

She frowned. "I can't imagine how he could know about it. We didn't live here when we were married, I was a schoolteacher in Austin. I don't remember mentioning it either."

"We'll check it out, anyway," Marshall said.

"It's about seven miles from here, and it will take you a long time to get there on foot," she warned. "I have several four-wheelers, though, if you'd like."

"Thanks, but the sound of the four-wheeler engines will scare off anyone trying to hide nearby," Sam said. "We'll stick to checking the area closest to the main living quarters on foot, first. We'll check the old ranch house later."

"Of course. That makes sense." Too bad her

father had sold the horses. Riding the ranch had been one of her favorite pastimes. Yet living here alone and raising a small son, she doubted she'd have been able to keep the horses anyway.

When she finished with the rough map, each of the rangers including Sam took a picture with their cell phones.

"Thanks. We'll head out now," Tucker said. He glanced at Sam. "You staying here?"

"Yeah." Sam walked them to the door. "Call me if you find anything."

"Will do." The guys headed outside. Sam closed the door behind them.

She busied herself at the sink, washing dishes. Sam refilled his coffee cup, then resumed his seat at the table. It took all her willpower not to glance over her shoulder to see if he was watching her.

Despite her silent promise to never get married again, she was keenly aware of Sam Hayward. His rugged good looks, his warm brown eyes, and his kindness and determination to keep her and Theo safe. She knew that the Texas Ranger would do the same for anyone in a similar position, but she was still touched by his steadfast presence. She knew Roy would have to go through Sam, and the other rangers, too, before he'd get to her.

Oddly, she enjoyed having a man to cook for. It had been just her and Theo for over a year now. She'd always imagined having a large family.

But that dream had been shattered when Roy had become physically abusive. And then was arrested for murder.

No, a large family of her own wasn't in her future. She had decided it would be best to focus on the blessings God had given her. A warm home, livestock to care for, and Theo.

She didn't need anyone or anything else.

As Mari washed and dried dishes, Sam did his best to keep from staring at her. He had wanted to head out with Tuck, Jackson and Marsh to scour the property, but leaving Mari and Theo alone was out of the question. The plywood-covered windows wouldn't stop a bullet, and they also limited her ability to see anyone approaching from outside.

But he should have asked one of the other guys to stay behind. This closeness to Mari was distracting.

"Will you play with me?" Theo asked.

"Ah, sure." He set his coffee aside and took the horse the young boy offered. "This one is a beauty—he looks like a thoroughbred. Does he have a name?"

"I call him Flash." Theo picked up another horse. "And this one is Speedo, because he's faster than Flash."

"I see." He had to give the kid credit for having a vivid imagination. "Those are great names."

Theo chatted more about his horses and how they were going to race each other again, soon.

"Sam, I need to head outside to gather eggs," Mari said. "I don't want to wait too long. The guys have been outside for a while now. I'm sure if anyone was hiding close to the house, barn or chicken coop, they'd have found him."

It was a good point. Still, he hesitated, then stood. "Maybe I should do that." He glanced pointedly at the shotgun. "You and Theo should be fine for a few minutes, right?"

She frowned. "You know how to gather eggs?"

He had a vague memory of doing that chore during those summers at Cameron's ranch. "Sure. How hard can it be?"

Arching a brow, she crossed to the pantry to pull out a crocheted basket with at least a dozen small egg pockets. The soft yarn was constructed to protect the eggs from slamming into each other. "You'll want to use this. Be careful not to break them even if the hens peck at you. I count on the income I get from selling eggs. It's not much, but it's something."

That gave him pause, but then he nodded. "I will."

The task was more difficult than he'd remembered and probably took him twice as long as it would have taken Mari. The heated chicken coop was warm enough, but the hens didn't like his intrusion. Mari had warned him about getting pecked, but he hadn't anticipated how badly those sharp beaks hurt.

When his basket was filled, he carried it inside and gratefully handed it to Mari. "Here you go."

"Thanks." She filled the sink with water, and carefully washed the eggs. Then she handed him the basket again. "One more pass-through should do it."

One more? He tried not to wince or look at his bloodied and scratched hands. "Got it."

The entire process gave him a better appreciation for Mari's grit and determination to provide for her son. He knew eggs weren't very expensive, so it wasn't like she made a ton of money off this chore. He imagined she sold cattle and chickens, too.

The idea of her scrimping by bothered him. And made him that much angrier with Roy Carlton.

They really needed to find and arrest the escaped convict ASAP.

After handing off the second basket of eggs to Mari, he washed up and texted the guys. See anything suspicious?

It took a moment for them to respond. One by one they checked in.

From Marsh. Clear to the west.

From Tuck. Clear to the north.

And Jackson. Nothing to the east.

The front of Mari's property faced south. He appreciated the guys spreading out in different directions. Should they go all the way to the original ranch house? If Roy Carlton didn't know about it, his accomplices probably didn't either.

And being seven miles away meant the shooter would have had to walk all that way. Or drive across the property. Driving meant leaving tire tracks behind. He made a mental note to check it out later, just to be extra cautious.

He still couldn't figure out why Roy wanted Theo in the first place. Money from selling acreage seemed to be the only answer. But at Mari pointed out, there had to be a buyer willing to pay.

Did Carlton already have a buyer?

The thought brought him up short. That hadn't occurred to him until now.

"Mari? Has anyone offered to buy the ranch from you or your father?"

She glanced up from where she was kneading bread. The yeasty scent made his mouth water. "Not recently, why?"

"When exactly?" he pressed.

She thought about it. "Maybe three years ago? I didn't pay that much attention because I was

going through a lot back then, having left Roy
and filing for divorce. And my dad didn't think
the buyer was serious."

"Did you father mention a dollar amount? Or
the guy's name?"

"No name, and the dollar amount was maybe
1.5 million, which is far less than what it's worth
on paper. But it sounded like my dad didn't believe the guy had the money or the ability to get
financing." She shook her head. "That's the biggest problem with people wanting to buy and fi-
nance ranches. You have to make enough of a
profit for a bank to agree to a large loan. Without
that, the sale likely wouldn't go through."

He was silent for a moment, wondering if she
would allow him to go through her dad's personal
paperwork to get more information.

"Why are you asking?" She put the lump of
bread dough aside.

"What if Roy had tried to grab Theo to force
you into selling to someone at a bargain basement
price?" He moved closer, keeping his voice low
so Theo couldn't hear. "That same person could
have helped Roy escape the hospital."

She frowned. "Even buying at a bargain basement price would take a significant amount of
money. Like I said, the guy offered 1.5 million.
And anyone who would pressure me into selling would likely not go to a bank for a loan,

which would mean they'd need to have that kind of money sitting around." She shook her head. "There has to be something else going on here."

"Maybe Roy wanted you to drive him across the border." He shrugged. "But that didn't work, so he thought shooting at you would force your hand."

"You said the shooter took off in a truck last night, but you couldn't get the license plate because it was covered in mud," she protested. "Why not use that to head to the Mexican border?"

It was another good point. He fell silent, filtering through additional theories.

But any way he looked at it, the entire situation didn't jell. Especially when factoring in the murder of Jeff Abbott.

When his phone rang, he quickly answered. "Tuck? What's going on?"

"Hey, I found some tire tracks not far from the spot where we believe Jeff Abbott was murdered. You may want to come out here to see for yourself."

He absolutely wanted to take a look. But did he dare leave Mari and Theo alone in the house? The guys hadn't stumbled across anyone lurking outside. He remembered the scene of the actual murder was roughly fifty yards away from where he'd found the garbage bag.

"Okay, I'll be right there." He stood and crossed to where Mari was cleaning the flour from her cutting board. "I need to check something out. Will you and Theo be okay for a few minutes?"

"Of course." Her smile didn't quite reach her eyes. She glanced at the shotgun she had near her pantry. "This time, I won't hesitate to shoot."

"Good." He hated the idea of her needing to take such drastic action, but he was proud of her willingness to protect herself and her son. "This shouldn't take long. Fifteen to twenty minutes at the most."

"Okay." She hesitated, then added, "I can make breakfast for the others, too, if they're hungry."

"Only if you let me reimburse you for the cost of bacon," he said. "Those guys eat like hounds."

This time, her smile brightened her eyes. "No need to worry about the bacon. We're not destitute. It's the least I can do for the way y'all are looking out for me. For us," she amended, glancing at Theo.

He wanted to insist but decided to worry about that later. Right now, he needed to get out to check out the tire tracks. Had the crime scene techs missed them? It was dark, so maybe.

"Keep the weapon close," he murmured. Then shrugged into his jacket, grabbed his hat and headed outside. He purposefully went out the front, scanning the area around the driveway. The curve in the driveway prevented him from seeing all the way to the road. No one was by the tree, though, so that was good.

He turned and rounded the corner of the house, heading down along the same path he'd taken the night before. It seemed like days ago, instead of mere hours. A lot had happened since he'd arrived and ultimately stayed at the Whistling Creek Ranch.

The thought had him making a mental note to have one of the guys stand guard over Theo and Mari so he could head back to the hotel long enough to shower and change his clothes.

He kept a keen eye out for anything he or the others may have missed, but there was nothing unusual. The sun was slowly warming the air, and he noticed the cattle were moving around more.

Several of them looked at him curiously as he walked by. They weren't exactly guard dogs, he thought with a grim smile.

He was more than halfway down to Whistling Creek when he heard the crack of gunfire.

Without hesitation, he spun on his heel and broke into a run, hoping and praying the shot had been fired by Mari and not someone else.

Like Roy Carlton.

SIX

Mari had finished the dishes when the kitchen window shattered seconds after her brain registered the sound of gunfire.

Not again!

She ducked, her heart pounding in her chest. That had been too close! Grabbing the shotgun, she ran into the living room to scoop Theo into her arms. Then she headed down the hall to her master bedroom, intending to use the closet for a hiding spot. It was the only place she could think of to buy time. Especially since the gunfire had come from the front of the house.

"The scary man is back," Theo sobbed.

She couldn't argue. "We're okay. Mr. Sam will be here soon." After yanking open the closet door, she stepped inside and set Theo on his feet.

"Mommy," he cried, clutching her legs. She hated how scared he was. No child should suffer this much terror and danger. "I want my Charlie!"

The stuffed dog was likely in the living room,

so going back for it was not happening. She held the shotgun with the muzzle pointing to the floor and pulled her phone from her pocket. She needed to call this in because she had no idea how far away Sam had been when the shooter had taken aim and fired at the house.

Was he close enough to have heard it? There was no way to know.

Fingers shaking, she dialed 911 with one hand.

"Hello, what is your emergency?"

"This is Mari Lynch at Whistling Creek Ranch." She did her best to remain calm despite the fact this was the second call like this she'd made in a handful of hours. "The gunman is back, he shot at me through the kitchen window."

"Are you safe?" The dispatcher asked.

"We're hiding in the closet of my room." Theo's sobbing ripped at her heart. "Please hurry. I'm afraid he'll come inside the house."

"Stay on the line with me. I've dispatched two deputies to your location."

It was the same pat answer she'd gotten earlier, and that response had taken far too long. Almost twenty minutes before those deputies arrived. Normally she loved living on the ranch, but not now.

Not when she and her son were in danger.

"I can't. He might come inside the house to find us. Just hurry." She disconnected the call and shoved the phone into her pocket. Then she gripped the shotgun with two hands and prepared herself mentally to fire at the first sign of danger.

She would not hesitate. Not this time.

It wouldn't help to think the worst. If she had Sam's personal cell number she'd call him. But she didn't. All she could do was to wait and pray.

Come on, Sam, where are you?

Theo's sobbing subsided, enabling her to hear better. She tried to tuck him behind her, but he wouldn't budge, gripping her legs so tightly she couldn't so much as take a step.

That was okay. If the intruder did get inside, there was no way she could miss at this close range.

But she desperately hoped it wouldn't come to that. She didn't want Theo to be even more traumatized than he was already.

Please, Lord Jesus, keep us safe in Your care!

One minute passed. Then another.

"Mari? Theo? Are you safe?"

Sam's voice was a welcome relief. Yet she didn't move out from their hiding spot. For all she knew the gunman was hiding inside somewhere, waiting to take one last shot.

"We're okay!" She shouted as loudly as she could. "We're hiding!" She didn't know how much to say in case the gunman was listening.

The last thing she wanted was to give their location away.

"Stay where you are!" Sam called.

She didn't respond, hoping the gunman would figure out that he was about to get caught. If he was hiding inside the house. In a way she hoped he was. She would be able to breathe easier once the gunman was found and arrested.

Roy? Or someone else? That was the tough question.

"Mommy? Is that Mr. Sam?" Theo asked with a loud sniffle.

"Yes." She didn't lower the weapon but glanced down at her son. "He's going to make sure we're safe. He won't let the scary man find us."

"I like Mr. Sam," Theo whispered.

His innocent words made her chest tighten. She was happy Theo had someone to look up to, but it was so wrong that her young son was frightened out of his mind.

She heard movement, doors opening and closing, floorboards creaking.

"Clear!" someone said.

"Clear!" Sam chimed in.

She understood Sam had at least one of his rangers with him. It didn't take long for Sam to come into the master suite. "Mari? Are you and Theo okay in there?"

"Yes." A wave of relief hit hard. A few minutes later, Sam opened the closet door. She slowly lowered the shotgun when she saw him. "Thank you for getting here so quickly."

"I shouldn't have left at all." Sam's grim expression softened when he glanced down at Theo. "Are you all right?"

Theo nodded, but then said, "I need Charlie."

"Oh, yes. Your stuffed dog. I'll get him." Sam lifted his gaze to her. "Pack a few things for you and Theo. We can't stay here."

She wanted to protest, but knew he was right. Yet that didn't mean it would be easy to go. She needed the ranch to be profitable for Theo. "I understand, but what about the livestock? I can't leave them to the elements."

Sam grimaced. "Do you have a neighbor who can help?"

"Tom Fleming lives on the next ranch with his wife, Irene, but he's in his midsixties." She nibbled her lower lip. "I hate to put more pressure on him. He has his own chores to do."

Sam held her gaze. "I can't tell you what to do about the ranch, Mari. But staying here isn't an option."

Letting out her breath in a heavy sigh, she nodded. "I'll call Tom. I helped him out last spring when his wife was ill. I'm sure he can help for a day or two."

"Good. Make it quick and then pack a bag."

"There's one last piece of plywood down-stairs," Jackson said. "I'll use it on the kitchen window."

"Thank you." Mari called Tom Fleming, grateful when he readily agreed to gather eggs and check on the cattle. She gave him a little information about the danger, only because he could hardly miss seeing the boarded-up windows.

"You and Theo are welcome to stay with us," Tom was quick to offer. Out here, neighbors helped each other when able.

"I don't want to put you and Irene in danger. The Texas Rangers are here and watching over me." It occurred to her that Tom could be in danger just by coming over to the property to help with her chores, so she added, "Make sure to keep your shotgun handy when you stop over. I doubt my ex-husband will attack you. It's me he wants, but I would feel better if you were armed."

"Will do. Be careful out there."

"Thanks." She ended the call, wondering if she had done the right thing by asking for Tom's help. If something bad happened to Tom or Irene, she'd feel awful.

"Mari?" Sam poked his head into the bedroom. "Ready?"

"Almost." She quickly pulled out a small suit-case and stuffed a change of clothing and toi-letries inside for her. Then ducked into Theo's room to do the same. She added some of his toys to help keep him busy, wherever they ended up staying.

Five minutes later, she had the suitcase and the shotgun in the kitchen, ready to go. Jackson and Sam were just finishing with the plywood.

"Charlie!" Theo grabbed the stuffed dog from the table and held it to his chest. "Can I bring him?"

"Of course." She forced a smile, then glanced toward Sam. "What's the plan?"

"Unfortunately, the shooter took out the tires on both SUVs," Sam said. "We'll need to borrow your four-wheelers."

She opened the junk drawer and pulled out the keys. "I have three of them. Is that enough?"

"We'll make it work." Sam took the keys. "I'll take you and Theo on one. Jackson will grab the other, meeting up with Tuck and Marsh. Let's go out the back."

She pulled on her coat, helped Theo with his, instructing him not to let go of Charlie. She held Theo's hand as she followed Sam through the house. Sam had both the suitcase and shotgun with him. Jackson stayed close behind. The late December breeze was chilly as they stepped outside. As if he owned the place, Sam headed straight for the barn where the four-wheelers were parked.

"These won't get us all the way to Fredericksburg which is slightly closer than Austin," she warned as she climbed up on the closest one. Sam lifted Theo up and placed him in her arms. Then he tucked the suitcase and shotgun on the storage space located in the back, strapping both items securely in place.

"We'll use that map you drew of the property to head to the original ranch house," Sam said. "We need to check it out anyway. And if no one has been there, it will be a good place to stay for a day or two."

She nodded. They could make it work.

The minor discomfort would be worth it to keep Theo safe.

Sam fired up the four-wheeler, relieved to note that Mari apparently kept up with making sure the ranch equipment was in working order. He'd half expected to find the battery was dead, or the engine filled with sludge gas, but it sounded great.

He nodded at Jackson, who shoved the barn door open before jumping on the second four-wheeler. Sam would have to go slow, having both Mari and Theo riding with him, so he'd given Jackson instructions to head to the creek to drop off a key to Tuck and Marsh, then head straight for the original ranch house. Sam wanted to be sure that he wasn't taking Mari and Theo into a trap.

Sam drove out of the barn first, followed by Jackson. But his fellow ranger hit the gas and sped ahead, anxious to join the other rangers.

It had occurred to Sam that the shooter must have been watching the ranch house, waiting for him to leave before striking out again. He kicked himself for leaving the south side of the property open, making the wrong assumption the shooter would hide out back.

A mistake he wouldn't make again.

The more attempts the gunman made against Mari, the more he believed the shooter had to be her ex-husband, Roy Carlton. Maybe this was all about simple revenge. Carlton held a grudge against Mari and wanted to take her out of the picture before escaping to Mexico.

The attempt to grab Theo was the only part that didn't fit with that scenario. Not that anyone claimed Roy Carlton was rational or logical. The guy should be on his way to Mexico by now, rather than making a grab for his son and shooting at Mari's home.

He drove slowly down the tree line toward Whistling Creek. Imagining Mari's rough sketch in his head, he waited until there was a break in the trees to head northwest.

Theo's tiny hands clutched his jacket, while

Mari held on to his shoulder. Under different circumstances, he would have enjoyed riding the property with them.

Up ahead he heard the roar of Jackson's four-wheeler. The guy had made it down to the creek in record time. He could imagine Jackson handing off the key to the third machine, then turning to reach the original ranch house well ahead of Sam.

He glanced over his shoulder at Mari, who appeared to be scanning their surroundings. Over the roar of the engine, he said, "Let me know if I go off course."

She nodded. "You're doing fine."

He hit a particularly hard bump, causing Theo to cry out in fear. He forced himself to slow down, despite the deep sense of urgency pushing at him to get Mari and Theo to safety.

Jackson was at the ranch house by the time they arrived. Sam parked his four-wheeler next to the empty one, grateful to see that there were no footprints or tire tracks in the slight dusting of snow around the building, other than Jackson's.

His fellow ranger came out of the house, waving them inside. "It's all clear."

"Thank the Lord Jesus," Mari whispered behind him.

He waited for her to slide off first. Once she had Theo in her arms, he hopped off and grabbed the suitcase and shotgun from the small cargo area. He led the way up to the house, scanning their surroundings. He could see why her grandfather had chosen the location, although it was much farther from the main highway. Maybe that had been an intentional move on his part.

It was cold inside, but he noticed Jackson had taken the time to build a fire in the wood-burning stove.

Mari stood holding Theo's hand, looking around curiously. "It's rather dusty, but otherwise it looks the same as the last time I was here."

"Good. That means no one has been inside recently." He was reassured by both the layer of dust and the lack of footprints in the snow.

Jackson's phone rang, and his buddy moved away to answer the call. Sam pulled his own phone, surprised to see there were two bars of service.

Not great, but not terrible. The biggest problem was their isolated location. Even if he called for backup, none would be forthcoming in anything close to a timely manner.

"I just got a call from our boss." Jackson turned back to Sam. "Owens has contacted the others, too. Unfortunately, we're not going to be able to stick around. He wants me to head to the hospital to interview more staff members about the night of Carlton's escape. Tucker is being sent to chat with the city manager and Marsh was told to follow up with the medical examiner on Abbott's autopsy."

"Go," Sam said without hesitation although he wished he could take a more active role in the investigation, too. "It's obvious no one has been in the area. We'll be safe here."

Mari's gaze held concern but she didn't argue. She took Theo closer to the warmth radiating from the stove and pulled some toys from the bag for him.

"I hate to leave you here," Jackson said, keeping his voice down so as not to alarm Theo. "But Owens has a point. Finding and arresting Roy Carlton is the quickest way to eliminate the danger to Mari and Theo."

He nodded. "I agree."

Jackson hesitated, then added, "Be careful. She's beautiful and the kid is cute, but you're on the brink of becoming emotionally involved."

Jackson wasn't telling him anything he didn't already know. "I hear you loud and clear."

"Do you?" Jackson arched a brow, flashing a skeptical gaze. "Why do I feel like it's already too late?"

"It's not. I'm fine." His denial was quick, but even he knew he wasn't being entirely honest.

Despite his best intentions, he had let Mari and Theo get too close. In his defense, it was

impossible to remain objective when an innocent woman and her young son were constantly
under fire from a ruthless gunman.

"Famous last words," Jackson shot back, before stepping outside. Minutes later, he was on
the four-wheeler and heading back to Mari's barn.

The interior of the original ranch house was
warming up nicely. Almost too cozy, with the
three of them staying here. He glanced at Mari,
crouched near her son. "I'm heading out to get
more wood."

She glanced up. "Okay. There's a woodpile
about fifty yards from the back door of the house.
We do have a gas furnace but I keep it really low
to preserve fuel. It would be nice to use the stove
for heat as much as possible. Oh, and I can head
down to the utility room to flip the breaker so
we have electricity. I generally keep it off during the winter."

"I'll check it out." He frowned, then added,
"You should keep the door locked, though. And
the shotgun handy."

"I will." Her green eyes held a steely determination. He thought about how she'd looked holding the gun ready while standing in the closet.

He wanted to step forward and gather her
close, but with Jackson's warning echoing in his
ear, he turned to head back outside.

There was barely a quarter inch of snow on the

ground. He wondered why it hadn't melted, but the wind coming from the north likely contributed to it sticking around.

He worked quickly, hauling split logs from the woodpile and neatly stacking them along the side of the house close to the back door. By the time he finished, he felt certain they'd have enough wood to heat the place for at least the next twenty-four hours.

They should have Roy Carlton in custody by then. Although it would help to identify his accomplices. One if not two people would have been involved in helping him escape.

He stomped the stray bit of snow from his boots as he rapped on the front door. As directed, Mari had locked it behind him.

"Hey." She opened the door to let him in. "Thanks for doing that."

"Of course." He shrugged out of his coat and removed his cowboy hat. Glancing in the living room, he saw Theo was curled up on the sofa with a blanket and his stuffed dog, Charlie. His eyes were drooping as if sleepy.

He followed Mari into the kitchen. "Does he usually take naps in the morning?"

"Never." She crossed her arms over her chest, watching her son for a long moment. "He was up early, though, and has been through a lot."

So had she. "I'm sorry. I wish I hadn't left you alone."

"This isn't your fault, it's Roy's." She turned away and opened a few cupboard doors. "There isn't much to eat as far as lunch and dinner goes. Canned soup and cans of beef stew are the best I can offer."

"That's okay, we'll survive." He frowned as she moved jerkily from one cupboard to the next poking through the supplies.

Then she abruptly stopped and placed her hands on the countertop, her head bowed as if struggling to hold herself together.

"Hey, don't fall apart now." He hoped his voice didn't betray his panic. "We're safe here."

"Are we?" Her voice was thick with anguish. "How long will it take before the gunman finds us here? A couple of hours?"

"Please, don't." Ignoring Jackson's warning, he crossed over to put his arm around her. "I promise I won't leave you. I'll stay close until Roy has been arrested."

To his surprise, she turned and stepped into his arms, burying her face against his chest. He cradled her close, whispering reassurances. It only took her a few minutes to pull herself together.

"Sorry about that." She sniffled and swiped at her eyes. "I didn't mean to cry on your shoulder."

"I'm here for you, Mari. No matter what you need." His own voice sounded husky to his ears.

"I wish—" She abruptly stopped and shook her head. Then she went up on her tiptoes to kiss his cheek.

He hadn't meant to take things any further, but somehow he'd captured her mouth in a warm kiss.

SEVEN

Sam's kiss warmed Mari's heart. It had been so long since she'd been held and kissed. Even though she knew Sam probably only intended to offer her comfort, she couldn't deny wishing for more.

Far too soon, Sam broke off the kiss. "I'm sorry," he murmured.

She frowned. "Why? Because you didn't want to kiss me?"

"What? No." He looked shocked, then chagrined. "But I did take advantage of our situation. And I shouldn't have."

His comment proved what she'd thought—that he wasn't interested in her as a woman. And wasn't that for the best?

"You didn't. I'm the one who almost fell apart. But I'll be okay." She straightened her shoulders and lifted her chin. Theo needed her to remain strong. To be able to provide for him. They would get through this.

She'd learned the hard way that being alone was better than being with the wrong man.

"Mari…" His voice trailed off as his gaze searched hers. "I care about you, very much. But I also need to keep you safe."

And those two things were mutually exclusive? Maybe. She didn't ask but forced a smile. "I understand."

She turned to grab the cans of soup, desperate to change the subject. "We'll have this for lunch and beef stew for dinner."

"Sounds great." He sounded as enthusiastic as if she'd offered him a four-course meal. "What can I do to help?"

"Nothing. I can manage." She rummaged in the cupboards for a saucepan. The gas stove worked well, and even though she didn't have money to spare, she'd turned the electricity back on, too.

Thanks to Roy, money was the least of her worries.

For a moment she felt herself sliding back into a sinkhole of despair. She and Theo didn't deserve this. Then again, God never said that His children wouldn't face challenges. But God did provide the strength and courage to overcome them.

She would do better in leaning on her faith to get through this.

When she noticed Sam going through some

of the cupboards, she turned to face him. "What are you looking for?"

"Something to wipe the dust off the table," he answered absently.

Why was he sticking so close? She'd feel better if he'd have stayed outside for a while longer.

"I can take care of it." She wasn't used to having help with basic household chores. "Sit down and relax."

He hesitated, then nodded as if sensing she needed space. After settling into the rocking chair next to the stove, he tipped his head back and closed his eyes.

Grateful to have him out of her way, she quickly rinsed the saucepan and then filled it with three cans of soup. She would have loved to have crackers or bread to go along with the meal, but that wasn't possible. She didn't keep perishable groceries here.

When she was finished with that, she began cleaning the kitchen counters, table and other surfaces. Staying busy helped to a certain extent. She wasn't afraid of Roy finding them here, not with Sam on guard.

Yet cleaning did not keep her from ruminating over Sam's heated kiss. And her instant response to his embrace. She'd acted like a starving woman wanting more.

How embarrassing.

Glancing at Theo, she debated waking him from his nap. His sleep schedule was going to be messed up if she allowed him to sleep too long.

Sam rose and fed more wood into the stove. The interior of the ranch house had warmed up nicely. She averted her gaze, thinking that being here with Sam was more intimate than earlier at the ranch house. Maybe because the boarded windows were a constant reminder of the danger.

Or maybe it was just the aftermath of his kiss. She really needed to find a way to get over it.

"Mommy?" Theo lifted his head, his brown hair sticking up on one side. "Where are we?"

"We took a ride on the four-wheeler, remember?" Having finished with the kitchen, she crossed over to sit beside him. "We're at the old house."

"Oh, yeah." He yawned widely and blinked adorably. "I remember now."

Maybe she shouldn't have mentioned how they'd been forced to leave to escape danger. He'd seemed to sleep peacefully without nightmares. But Theo didn't ask anything more as he scooted off the sofa. "I hav'ta go to the bathroom."

"This way." She glanced at Sam. "Will you stir the soup please?"

"Of course." He finished with the wood stove, brushing the bark from his fingers.

By the time Theo had finished and washed his

hands, she heard a voice from the kitchen. She followed her son back to the main living space, not surprised to discover Sam was on the phone.

Another reminder that he was here working the case of her escaped ex-husband. Not hanging out for fun and games.

"Thanks for the update," Sam said before ending the call.

"Did they find him?"

"Not yet." He looked as if he might say more but held back when Theo darted toward him.

"Will you play with me, Mr. Sam?"

"Sure. But I think it may be time to eat lunch."

Mari nodded, crossing to the stove. It was early, but that was okay. "Sam, will you grab a pillow for Theo to sit on? I'll dish up the soup."

A minute later, they were seated at the table. She took Theo's hand and bowed her head. "Dear Lord Jesus, we are grateful for this food You have provided. Please continue to keep us safe in Your care and give the Texas Rangers the wisdom and strength to find the truth. Amen."

"Amen," Sam echoed.

"Amen. Can't I have bread with my soup?" Theo asked with a frown.

She had the bread dough rising back at the house, but going back wasn't an option. "I'm afraid not. But chicken noodle is your favorite, right?"

Theo's lower lip stuck out. "But I like bread."

She swallowed a sigh. It wasn't his fault they were making do here at her grandfather's ranch house.

"I love this soup," Sam declared. "It's good without bread."

Theo eyed him for a moment, then mimicked Sam's movements. It made her heart squeeze to realize how much her son looked up to Sam in just the short time he'd spent with them.

Then she worried about how Theo would react once the threat of Roy had been eliminated and Sam wasn't around any longer.

Sam did his best to keep Theo preoccupied as they finished lunch. The kid was impressionable, and that was a good thing.

But it did make him wonder what Mari and Roy's life was like prior to her divorce. He didn't want to pry into her personal life, but it was obvious Theo didn't remember his father very well.

If at all.

"I'll clean up," he offered when they were finished.

"Are you always this helpful?" she asked with a frown. "I mean, most men leave kitchen duty to women."

"My grandmother would give me the stink eye

from heaven if I didn't offer to help," he joked. "She always made Granddad pitch in."

"That surprises me," Mari admitted. "Especially from that generation."

"It's common courtesy." He didn't add that there wasn't much of anything else to do. Keeping his voice down, so Theo wouldn't overhear, he added, "What do you think of taking Theo outside to build a small snowman?"

She hesitated. "Is it safe enough?"

"I think so, if we stay in the backyard." They had his sidearm and her shotgun. He didn't anticipate that Roy or his accomplices would find them there so quickly. "Just for a short time. Enough for him to burn off some excess energy."

"Okay." She smiled. "That would be great."

The task of washing their dishes didn't take long, then they headed outdoors. He was surprised at how much fun they had playing in the snow. Theo was all about building a big snowman, but they had to make it a small one as there wasn't that much to work with.

"He's a mini-snowman," Mari declared. "Perfect size, Theo, don't you think?"

"Yep." Theo stuck his tongue out and licked the snowman's head. Sam was taken aback but Mari bit her lip as if holding back a laugh. "He doesn't taste good, though," Theo announced.

"We don't eat or lick them, we just look at

them." Mari shook her head ruefully then slapped her gloved hands together to get the excess snow off. "Let's go, Theo. It's time to head back inside."

"Aw, do we hav'ta?"

"Yes. You're shivering," she pointed out.

Sam hadn't noticed, although now that he looked at the boy, it was so obvious he was chilled to the bone. "You heard your mother. We need to get inside."

Theo stared at him for a moment as if gauging if he should argue, but then dashed toward the door. "I win!"

"How is it that I'm more exhausted after building that snowman than he is?" he asked as they went inside.

"Trust me, it's one of life's many mysteries." Mari sighed. "Theo is proof that energy is wasted on the youth."

The rest of the day passed without incident. He played with Theo as Mari warmed up the canned beef stew for dinner. As dusk fell, Mari had turned the kitchen light on. He'd asked her to flip it off, preferring to sit in the darkness with only the faint glow from the wood-burning stove as light.

If Roy or his accomplices had found out about the house, it made sense that they'd wait to strike at night. No doubt having learned from their earlier mistake in taking a shot at Mari through the kitchen window in broad daylight. He didn't want Mari or Theo to be an easy target.

"I'm going to walk the perimeter," he said when they'd finished eating. "Shouldn't take longer than ten to fifteen minutes."

"Okay." She glanced at the shotgun he'd propped in the kitchen corner. "We'll be fine."

He settled his hat on his head, shrugged into his coat and headed outside. The darkness wasn't complete thanks to the reflection of the moon and stars against the snow. He stood for a moment, listening intently. Then he stepped away from the house and began to walk.

There were no footprints in the snow beyond the spot where he and Jackson had parked the four-wheelers. He hesitated, wondering if he should stick closer to the house, but then remembered how the gunman had used the tree for cover prior to shooting Mari's living room window.

He hiked in a circle, scouting any area a gunman could use as a nest. The good news was that there were no lights inside to make it easier for anyone to aim at Mari or Theo.

Not that he wouldn't try. Sam had to assume at this point that the gunman was feeling desperate.

After making a circle around the property, he headed back inside, well within the fifteen-minute time frame.

"Anything?" Mari asked as he stomped snow off his boots.

"All clear." He hiked a brow when he noticed she'd made a pallet on the floor near the wood-burning stove. "Are you and Theo sleeping in here?"

"For now." She grimaced. "I'm not sure how much gas we have in the LP tank. It's better if we use gas heat at a bare minimum."

"Sure thing." He didn't mind sleeping on the floor. Far better for Mari and Theo to use the sofa. "Whatever works."

He took a moment to bring in more wood for the stove, enough to last the night. He was hoping for an update from the guys, but so far they hadn't learned very much. Marsh had called to let him know the medical examiner had declared Jeff Abbott's death a homicide. He had been killed by the shotgun blast at close range. And Jackson had mentioned how one of the hospital employees had noticed a blue minivan leaving the parking garage shortly after the nurse had found Carlton's room empty, and the deputy locked in the bathroom with his own cuffs.

He'd hoped for more, but every small piece of information would help build the big picture.

Even though the convict should never have escaped in the first place.

Mari made hot chocolate out of water, which

Theo loved. Then she changed Theo into his superhero footie pajamas. Sam listened as Mari re-
cited a bedtime story from memory, then tucked
a quilt around Theo for added warmth. It didn't
take long for the little boy to fall asleep.

"Should I lift him onto the sofa?" he asked in
a whisper.

Mari nodded. When that was done, she made
sure his dog Charlie was within reach, then
moved over to the kitchen table so their talking
wouldn't disturb him.

"Can you fill me in on what's going on?" she
asked.

"We haven't learned as much as we'd hoped,"
he admitted. "Abbott's cause of death is no surprise. And they're following a few leads from
the hospital."

"I just don't understand any of this," Mari
whispered.

"I know." He reached out to take her hand. "I
wish I could tell you more. I'm sure we'll have
more leads by morning."

She stared at their clasped hands for a moment,
then gently pulled away. Her hot chocolate was
gone, but she held on to the mug as if it were a
lifeline. "What concerns me the most is that Roy
isn't a nice man," she whispered.

He frowned. "You mean because he murdered
Hank George?"

She shook her head but didn't say anything. A chill snaked down his spine.

"He hurt you?" Sam pressed. "Physically hurt you and Theo?"

"Me, not Theo." She stared into her empty mug for a long moment before lifting her head. The anguish in her eyes hit hard.

"How badly?"

She sighed and shook her head, dropping her gaze again. "It started with shouting and swearing, nonstop comments about how useless I was and how he never should have married me."

It was all Sam could do to sit calmly, as she described the abuse she'd endured. When she didn't add anything more, he asked, "When did it turn physical?"

"About a year after Theo was born." She turned to look at her sleeping son. "I started to stand up for myself, and he slapped me." She grimaced. "I should have left right then and there, but I didn't. Not until he hit me a second time."

"I hate that you had to go through that."

"My fault for marrying him." She set her empty mug aside. "I packed up Theo and went home to Whistling Creek. My dad wanted to beat Roy to a pulp, but I told him that wouldn't solve anything." A faint smile creased her features. "But my dad did come with me to get the rest of our things and brought his shotgun along, too. Roy stood back and let me take whatever I wanted without uttering a single objection."

Good for her dad, he thought. And wished he'd been around to help back then. "I'm glad. Good riddance. You're far better off without him."

"Yes, I know." Her brow furrowed. "Roy had some nerve trying to kidnap Theo."

"We'll find him." He tried to sound confident, although it was not reassuring that Carlton had eluded them even this long. "One thing Jackson learned is that a hospital staff member noticed a blue minivan leaving the parking lot shortly after your ex-husband escaped."

She looked up at him. "Really? You think Roy was inside?"

"It's a lead." As if on cue his phone rang and Jackson's name popped up on the screen. Still keeping his voice low, he answered, "What's up, Jackson?"

"Will you ask Mari if the name Cindy Gorlich means anything to her?"

He settled his gaze on her. "Mari? Do you know a Cindy Gorlich?"

"No, why?"

"That's a negative, Jackson. What role does Gorlich have in this?"

"She works as a nurse and reported her blue minivan stolen. I've interviewed her and she claims she told one of the sheriff's deputies about the theft, but I can't find anyone who admitted to talking to her."

"That's interesting. Do you think she's lying?"

"I don't know," Jackson said. "Keep in mind, the sheriff's department already has egg on their face over Carlton's escaping in the first place. Deputy Erickson admitted to getting too close to Carlton, allowing him to grab his sidearm. From there, it was easy enough to force Erickson into the bathroom and use his own cuffs to restrain him."

The story sounded worse every time he heard it. "So, what, you think they're covering up another error by not coming forward with the stolen vehicle report?"

"Why not?"

"Yeah, that's possible." He hoped heads would roll at the sheriff's department after this fiasco but he wouldn't bank on it. "Have you dug into Gorlich's background?"

"We're doing that now. No flags yet. But I thought you should know. And we were wondering if it was possible that Carlton was having an affair with Cindy Gorlich prior to his arrest."

"Hang on." He lowered the phone. "Are you aware of Roy having any girlfriends after your divorce?"

"No." Mari frowned. "If Roy was seeing someone, I didn't know anything about it." She paused, then added, "Honestly, I may have been tempted to warn his girlfriend about his physical abuse, for her sake. I would not have wanted anyone else to suffer either."

He believed her. "Thanks." He lifted the phone. "Mari has no knowledge of her ex having a girlfriend. But maybe canvassing the area would come up with someone who saw them together."

"More than two years ago?" Doubt laced Jackson's tone. "Most people can barely remember what they ate for dinner the night before."

"We have to try." Sam's face flushed, as he added, "Sorry. I would be there helping if I could."

"Yeah, yeah. Coming from the guy who has the gravy assignment," Jackson teased. "We'll ask around and dig a little deeper. How are things by you?"

"Quiet. We're good. Keep me updated, Jackson."

"You know it." His fellow ranger disconnected the call.

As Sam lowered his phone, he thought about Jackson's comment. For a gravy assignment, he was feeling mighty tense.

The responsibility of keeping Mari and Theo safe was heavy on his shoulders. He'd made mistakes in the past, one that had nearly cost his fellow rangers' lives.

He refused to make a similar mistake in judgment this time. He needed to stay hypervigilant in his quest to protect Mari and Theo.

EIGHT

Roy likely had a girlfriend. Mari wasn't sure why the news bothered her. She'd been thankful to have him out of her life, and to be granted sole custody of Theo. What her ex did in his free time was his own business.

Some women were attracted to men in prison, or maybe Roy had started seeing someone while they were still married. After everything that had transpired in the past twenty-four hours, she wouldn't put anything past him.

"You should get some sleep," Sam murmured. "Take the sofa with Theo. I'll sleep on the floor."

Startled by the offer, she nodded. Although she shouldn't have been surprised. Sam had been nothing but a gentleman and their steadfast protector during this nightmare. She had no doubt that he'd risk his life for her and Theo, if needed.

She prayed it wouldn't come to that. The Texas Rangers and the local police were searching for her ex. Roy couldn't hide forever.

Especially if he continued to seek revenge by coming after her and Theo. Or kidnapping their son for ransom. Or whatever he was up to.

"Good night." She stood and crossed to the sofa. Theo was sleeping on one end. She picked up the edge of the quilt and slid underneath so that her legs were stretched out alongside her son's.

The warmth from the wood-burning stove helped her to relax. They were safe here. And tomorrow? She winced, thinking about her ranch chores that Tom Fleming would need to do for her, in addition to his own.

Maybe they could head back to the main ranch house just long enough for her to check the cattle to make sure they had enough water and to gather eggs. With the four-wheeler, it wouldn't take that much time. And that way, she could grab additional food from her fridge and pantry.

Satisfied to have a plan, she closed her eyes and tried to sleep. Yet she was keenly aware of Sam moving around the living room, adding more wood to the fire before stretching out on the pallet she'd made on the floor.

His kiss had been wonderful. The moment that thought crossed her mind, she did her best to ignore it. Remembering their brief embrace would not help her fall asleep.

Just the opposite.

She silently prayed for God to continue watching over her, Sam and Theo. Between the prayer and the cozy atmosphere she drifted off to sleep.

Several times during the night, Sam added wood to the stove for added warmth. She doubted the floor was comfortable, but when she heard him softly snoring, she couldn't help but smile.

By the time the first rays of dawn beckoned on the horizon, Sam was up and moving around in the kitchen. Theo was still asleep, so she carefully disentangled herself from the sofa and quilt, then joined Sam.

"Good morning," she whispered.

"Morning." His smile warmed her heart. "Did you sleep okay?"

"About as well as you did. But thanks for keeping the stove going. That was nice."

"Anytime." He glanced around the kitchen. "No way to make coffee, huh?"

She chuckled at the wistful expression on his face. "There is an old-fashioned percolator here. I'll see if I can find it." She paused, then added, "I'm not sure the coffee that was left here is much good, though. It's probably stale."

"I'm not picky." He leaned against the counter, and she was keenly aware of how he watched as she silently checked various cabinets for the percolator. If things were different…

But they weren't.

The percolator was in the last cabinet she checked. She set it on the counter and began setting it up. Sam watched the process with interest.

"We've been spoiled by technology, haven't we?" he said in a low, wry tone.

"For sure." She found the coffee grounds in the fridge and filled the metal filter of the percolator. "One thing about old technology, it doesn't break down as easily."

"True," Sam agreed.

"Mommy?" Theo sat up on the sofa, rubbing his eyes. "I'm hungry."

"I know." She waved at the percolator. "You'll know when the coffee is ready. I need to take care of Theo."

"Go ahead," he said with a nod. "I'll grab more wood from the back door, too."

She wanted to ask if that was necessary, since she didn't think they'd need to stay much longer, but held her tongue. He was the expert. And she also knew his fellow rangers would call the minute they had Roy in custody.

After getting Theo washed up and changed into regular clothes, taking a few minutes to freshen up herself, she returned to the kitchen with her son.

"I found a container of oatmeal," Sam said. To her surprise he already had a pan of water warming up on the stove. "Figured that would work well for breakfast."

"No oatmeal," Theo pouted. "I want eggs and bacon."

She stifled a sigh. "Not today. But I can make another cup of hot chocolate if you'd like."

Theo's eyes widened and he nodded eagerly. "Yay! Hot chocolate!"

She'd hoped that would distract him from the oatmeal, which she knew wasn't her son's favorite. But if he was hungry enough, he'd eat it.

"You haven't heard anything from the other rangers?" She glanced at Sam questioningly.

"Not yet." He shrugged. "It's still early, though."

It was early in the morning, barely seven thirty, but Roy had been on the run for what seemed like forever. She bit her lip and told herself to be patient.

"I was hoping we could head back to the ranch house, just briefly." She stirred the oatmeal. "I want to be able to gather more eggs, check the cattle and maybe grab more food if we're going to be here for a while."

"I don't know if that's a good idea," Sam hedged. "We're safe here."

They were, but she had her livestock to consider. She dropped the subject for now, concentrating on finishing their makeshift breakfast of oatmeal and hot chocolate.

Theo squirmed on the pillow in his seat as she set their meal on the table. "Wait until we say grace," she warned when he reached for his hot chocolate. "Besides, it's too hot."

With an exaggerated sigh, he sat back. "Hurry up."

"We need to take time to express our gratitude," Sam said.

"What does that mean?" Theo asked.

She took Theo's hand. "It means we give thanks to our Lord Jesus for providing this food we are about to eat. And we also thank the Lord for keeping us safe. Amen."

"Amen," Sam echoed.

"Amen," Theo said. "Now can we eat?"

She couldn't help but laugh. He was still too young to fully grasp the idea of God and faith. But she was touched that Sam had participated in every prayer.

Supporting her in so many small yet important ways.

It occurred to her this partnership was what her parents had experienced. She and her dad had been devastated over losing her mother. But that loss had brought them closer together, too.

Until she'd married Roy, that is. Her dad had never liked him. Less so after she'd come home with Theo sporting a bruised lip and cheek.

They ate in silence for a few minutes.

"Have you considered my request to head back?" she finally asked.

He grimaced. "I don't know if we should. I would offer to go, but I can't leave you and Theo here alone."

"I'm sure the gunman has figured out we're not staying there anymore," she pointed out.

"Yeah, that's kind of what I'm afraid of," Sam admitted. "They may decide to expand their search of the ranch. I'm sure this house is still listed on the title."

She hadn't considered that. "It is, yes."

"I'll call Tucker when we're finished. See if there's been an update in the case," he said.

She nodded, masking her disappointment. She didn't want to take Theo into danger. But the meager supply of canned goods wouldn't last long. And Theo would whine over having soup again for lunch without bread or crackers.

When they finished eating, she filled the sink with soapy water. Sam moved into the living room to make his call. She strained to eavesdrop but couldn't hear much over Theo's chattering.

"I wanna play with my dump trucks," he said, shooting her a reproachful look. "How come you didn't pack them?"

There hadn't been time, and they were too big. She glanced at him, striving for patience. "I'm sorry I couldn't bring them along, but you have your horses, right? Play with those for now."

He thrust his lower lip out stubbornly. "I want my trucks."

She did her best not to snap at him. He wasn't old enough to understand. And she didn't want to remind him of the danger that had caused them to come here in the first place. "Maybe later."

"Show me your horses," Sam said. "Flash and Speedo, right?"

"Right!" Theo ran to the living room.

She met Sam's gaze over her son's head. "Thanks."

He smiled briefly, then said, "We can make a short trip to the ranch house. The sheriff's department had a deputy watching the place all night. No sign of any intruders."

That was good news. "Thanks so much." She almost asked if they couldn't just stay at the main house but decided not to push it. She took a moment to call Tom Fleming to let him know she'd be there to do the morning chores so he wouldn't have to bother, then finished the dishes. She let them dry in the sink, anxious to be on their way.

When she glanced toward her son, her heart squeezed as she saw how Sam was playing along with Theo, pretending to ride the horses across the pallet still covering the floor.

He was so good with her son. But this was also

a temporary situation. Easy to help keep a kid occupied when you weren't the child's parent on a full-time basis.

Yet watching them play only made her wish for something she'd never have.

A loving husband and more children.

Sam hoped and prayed he wasn't making a huge mistake by taking Mari and Theo back to the main house. According to Tuck, the deputy hadn't seen anyone lurking around, which was good.

Unfortunately, the rest of the news wasn't nearly as reassuring. There was still no sign of Roy Carlton, the missing blue minivan or a dark truck with mud-covered license plates.

How many accomplices did Carlton have, anyway? One? Two? A handful?

No, it was hard to imagine the guy having more than one or two people helping him. And when they figured out who those individuals were, they'd be tossed in jail right alongside Carlton for aiding and abetting a fugitive.

"What time should we head out?" Mari asked.

"Soon." He set Flash aside and rose to his feet. "But I need to walk the perimeter again, first."

"Play horsey with me," Theo protested.

"I will for a little while," Mari said, dropping down beside her son. "Mr. Sam has work to do."

He shrugged into his coat and placed his hat on his head before heading outside. The early morning light was bright, making him squint. Without hesitation, he made the same loop as he had last night, noticing there were plenty of wildlife tracks in the snow, white tail deer, foxes and coyote.

And thankfully, no human footprints other than his own.

He vacillated between leaving Mari and Theo here while he did the chores and taking them along. When Mari and Theo had been washing up and changing clothes, he'd taken stock of the food situation. The lack of canned goods and other items had convinced them a short trip back to the ranch house was in order.

He'd tried to convince Jackson, Tucker and Marshall to meet him at the ranch, but they were still following up on leads related to the investigation.

Satisfied their current location was secure, he headed back inside the house. Theo was arguing with Mari about wanting his trucks. Without a television or any other electronics to keep him occupied, the little boy was growing more insistent about having the rest of his toys.

"We'll take that trip up to the ranch house now," he said, interrupting Theo. "Make a list of the items you need."

"I have entered them in the notes section of my phone." Mari smiled and stood. "Thanks for doing this, Sam. I appreciate it."

"It's not a problem." He waited patiently for Mari to get Theo in his winter gear. Despite his excitement to get out of the house, he wiggled so much it was no easy task to get him in his coat, hat, mittens and boots.

And she sighed when he insisted on taking Charlie, his stuffed dog, along for the ride.

When the little boy was finally dressed, Sam led the way out back to where he'd left the four-wheeler. He jumped on first, starting the engine, then hopped off and helped Mari and Theo get situated.

"Ready?" he asked, glancing over his shoulder. Mari was holding on to the sides of his jacket, with Theo snuggled between them.

"As ever," she shot back.

Like yesterday, he took it slow, minimizing the bouncing along for their sake. The roar of the engine seemed incredibly loud in the otherwise peaceful setting.

There were several four-wheeler tracks along the ground, but he knew that he and Jackson had left them behind. Besides, he was certain he'd have heard anyone else out there on one of these things.

But all had been quiet last night.

For Mari and Theo's sake, he prayed the peace would last, and the gunman would focus his efforts elsewhere.

It took fifteen minutes for the ranch house to come into view. He drove up the hill along the tree line, sweeping his gaze over the area. The cattle, barn and chicken coop all looked undisturbed. So much so, he worried Mari's neighbor hadn't come out to take care of the afternoon chores after they'd left.

If Mari noticed anything amiss, she didn't mention it. She clung to him as they navigated the rocky terrain, reminding him of their heated kiss.

Don't go there, he silently warned himself. *Stay focused!*

He pulled to a stop beside the cattle. "Do you want to check the water level now?" he asked.

"Yes, please." She scrambled off the four-wheeler and ducked beneath the plank fence. The placid faces of the cows turned to look at her curiously as she spoke to them.

"How are you doing out here? Warm enough, I hope." She talked to them as if they were pets. "Looks like you have plenty of water. Go on, now, shoo!" She waved her arms. At first the cows simply stared at her, then began ambling around the pasture as if knowing this was their daily exercise routine.

"I'll walk up to the chicken coop," she said, waving him off.

He hesitated, then nodded. He knew from his brief experience in gathering eggs that the chickens would put up a squawking fuss if anyone had tried to hide in there.

Holding on to Theo with one hand, he drove up along the fence until he was next to the chicken coop. Then he climbed down and lifted Theo up and onto his feet.

"Stay close. We won't be here for long," he said.

"Okay." Theo ran over and climbed up so that he stood on the lower plank of the fence. The kid had been so quick and agile that Sam figured he'd done it before.

He continued scanning the paddock and outbuildings. Seeing nothing amiss, he joined Theo at the fence.

"My Pop Pop had horses," Theo said in a wistful tone. "But he had to sell them to make money."

"I'm sorry to hear that." He wondered how long ago that had been.

"I miss Pop Pop," Theo said. Then the kid looked up at him. "Are you going to be my daddy?"

Whoa, where had that come from? He scrambled for an acceptable answer. "I'm afraid not. Your mommy has to find a man she loves and get married for you to have a new daddy."

"Why?" Theo's brow furrowed. "Why can't you just be my daddy?"

He didn't have an answer for that one, but thankfully Mari emerged from the chicken coop. She must have had another of those knitted basket things in there, because she carried one full of eggs. "There's your mom. Now we can go inside and get some of your toys."

"Okay." Thankfully, Theo dropped the subject of Sam becoming his daddy. The kid jumped down from the fence and ran over to his mother. "Mr. Sam said we can go inside to get more toys."

"I heard him." Mari smiled. She looked so happy to be back home, doing mundane chores, that he wondered if he was being overprotective by not allowing them to stay here.

He turned away, calling himself all kinds of a fool to let her mess with his head. This was a brief visit long enough to stock up on food and toys for Theo.

Walking to the back door, he frowned when he realized it wasn't locked. Then again, they had left in a hurry the day before.

"Stay behind me," he cautioned, pulling the door open. He eased his weapon from its holster and stepped across the threshold. A horrible scent washed over him, causing him to take a hasty step back, bumping into Mari.

"What's wrong?"

"You can't go inside." He glanced over his shoulder, half expecting to hear gunfire. "Get Theo onto the four-wheeler. Hurry!"

She looked as if she might argue but took her son's hand. "Come with me, Theo."

For once, the kid didn't argue. Sam pulled the door open again and cautiously stepped inside. He made his way past the bedroom doors, frowning at the complete disarray in both Mari's and Theo's rooms. It seemed as if someone had searched the place. Looking for what, he wasn't sure. Sam came to an abrupt halt when he saw a man lying on the floor in front of the wood-burning stove.

Roy Carlton. Killed by a bullet to the center of his forehead.

NINE

Cradling Theo on her lap, Mari shivered as she waited for Sam to emerge from the house. Other than the sound of mooing and munching hay from the cattle, she didn't hear anything suspicious.

Yet there had been a reason Sam had refused to let her enter her home. And she knew it couldn't be anything good.

"I wanna get down," Theo whined.

"We're waiting for Mr. Sam." She tried to mask her fear of what was taking him so long. "He'll be here soon."

After what seemed like eons but was only about ten minutes, Sam stepped out of the house, his expression grim. "Marshall is on the way."

"Why?" She held his gaze. "Is there a reason I can't go inside to get food and more toys for Theo?"

"Mari." He came closer, his gaze dropping momentarily to Theo before looking at her. "I have some bad news. Roy is—gone." Despite the mild word, she knew he really meant dead.

Roy was dead? She was ashamed of the sense of relief that washed over her. Even though Roy was Theo's father, she was glad he was no longer a threat.

"And someone left him inside," Sam continued.

Wait, what? She gaped in horror. "Who?"

"I don't know." He rested his hand on her knee. "I'm as frustrated and upset as you are. We had a deputy stationed outside, watching the place. I can't begin to fathom how this happened."

A deputy had been there while someone killed Roy? No, she realized the murder must have happened elsewhere, and Roy's body placed here. Why? To incriminate her? That made no sense. It would be easy to prove she was with Sam the entire time.

"I don't understand what's going on," she whispered.

"I know. I wasn't expecting this either." Sam swept the area with his keen gaze. "I think someone searched your room and Theo's, but there's no one there now. I doubt the killer is hanging around. I'm sure he dumped Roy, searched the place then got out of here as quickly as possible. Yet I need you to stay alert."

She shook her head as a wave of helplessness washed over her. At first she'd thought the danger was over now that Roy was gone. But clearly,

Sam didn't feel the same way. And why search her and Theo's rooms?

"You think whoever did this will continue to come after us?"

"That's exactly right. Your ex was left here for a reason. Either to send a message to you or to whoever Roy was working with."

First Jeff Abbott was murdered and left on her property and now Roy. She bit hard on her lower lip to keep from losing control. All she wanted was to run her ranch, caring for the livestock and supporting her son.

But this? Why was she being dragged into this mess?

Unless...her blood ran cold. Had Roy told someone dangerous that she knew something? Key information that could be used against them? Maybe information that was thought to be hidden in their rooms?

It seemed the only logical explanation. Not that any of this came across as remotely logical.

She heard Sam talking on the phone and realized he was speaking with someone within the sheriff's department. He was polite yet pointed in relaying his annoyance at how a dead body had been left inside her home while it was supposedly being watched by a deputy.

"Please do," Sam said in a curt tone. "We'll be waiting for you."

Outside? She glanced down at Theo in concern. She could handle the cold weather, but her son would get chilled if they stayed out here much longer.

"I'm sorry. I'll get you and Theo warmed up as soon as possible," Sam said, reading her thoughts. "I can't leave until I can hand the crime scene over."

"I understand." She drew in a deep breath. "I guess we can head into the barn."

He hesitated, glancing around the area behind her ranch house again. "Please stay here for a little while longer. Marsh should be here soon. I caught him when he was on the road heading to Austin."

She nodded in agreement. Being alone in the barn with Theo wouldn't provide the sense of safety that came from sticking close to Sam. She wished she'd brought her shotgun along, but it hadn't seemed necessary.

Obviously, a wrong assumption.

Danger still lurked behind every corner. Not from Roy himself but from whatever he'd gotten himself involved with. At least she knew now why her ex hadn't made his way down to the Mexican border.

"How long has Roy been…" Her voice trailed off.

"I can't say for sure. We'll need the medical examiner to give us that information." Sam paused, then added, "He still could have been the shooter taking out your living room and kitchen windows. I plan to make sure his hands and clothing are tested for gunshot residue, to help answer that question."

"Okay." The way he spoke so calmly of evidence and clues helped keep her calm. Maybe they'd learn something from this that would put an end to the danger.

Yet she couldn't deny being angry with Roy for dragging her and Theo into this in the first place. Ironic that she'd been safe the entire time he was in prison, only to be smack in the center of danger when he'd escaped.

"Marsh is out front." Sam glanced up from his phone. "Let's take the four-wheeler around."

She nodded, scooting back to give Sam room to jump onto the seat. He hit the gas and drove around the side of the building closest to the tree line that led to the creek. The trip didn't take long, and she was glad to see Marshall standing outside his SUV.

"What happened with the other SUVs that were damaged by gunfire?" she asked, as Sam agilely hopped down.

"We were able to change the tires of one SUV, the other was towed to Fredericksburg," Sam said, reaching over to pick up Theo, then setting him on his feet. He helped her down, too. She felt a little ridiculous standing there with a crocheted basket of eggs but she wasn't going to waste them.

"Ms. Lynch." Marshall gave her a solemn nod. "I'm sorry to hear about your ex-husband."

She didn't know what to say to that, so she simply shrugged. "I hope you find the person responsible."

"We will." Marsh turned to Sam. "You cleared the house?"

"Yes. The two bedrooms had been searched, and of course you know what else we found." Sam tipped his head toward Theo. "The lack of blood indicates he wasn't killed there. The sheriff's department is sending a couple of deputies out too. They had someone out front watching the place."

Marsh hiked a brow and shook his head. "They're really not batting a thousand, are they?"

"Not at all. The deputy claimed he only left for a couple of bathroom breaks." Sam's expression turned thoughtful. "Do you think one of them is dirty? Maybe being paid to look the other way?"

"It's possible. First a deputy allows Roy to escape from the hospital, then a deputy is supposedly on guard duty while a dead body is dumped inside." Marshall sighed. "It's a stretch that the deputy assigned to watch the place is involved.

That seems rather obvious. But I agree, the sheriff's department is not looking good. There may be someone inside setting both of these deputies up for failure."

She shivered and not from the cold. A deputy working for the bad guys? Pulling strings and allowing Roy to escape, and then to be murdered? How could she and Theo possibly be safe if one of them was dirty? She tried to remember the name of the deputy who'd responded that first night. Oh, yes, Deputy Strawn. He'd seemed concerned and had taken her statement along with pictures of the window. Hard to imagine he would be involved.

From now on, she decided she would only trust the rangers. Especially Sam.

She and Theo would be safe with God and Sam Hayward watching over them.

After finding Roy Carlton's dead body, Sam had cleared the rest of the house. The two tossed bedrooms bothered him, but it could be that the shooter was looking for something to use to implicate Mari in Roy's death.

He'd initially intended to take Mari and Theo back to the original ranch house, but now he wasn't so sure if that was the right way to go.

He'd felt certain that Roy had been the one shooting at her. But his murder, so much like Jeff

Abbott's, gave Sam pause. Obviously someone was eliminating those involved in the original murder of Austin City Manager Hank George.

What role Abbott had played was unclear, but Roy had been arrested, charged and found guilty in a court of law. After spending two full years behind bars—the trial hadn't happened until more than a year after his arrest—he'd managed to escape.

Only to be murdered and left here on Whistling Creek Ranch. Had the goal been to scare Mari? Possibly.

As if she needed another reason to be afraid.

"You should know Jackson has another lead," Marsh said in a low voice. "A staff member who cleans the emergency department, guy by the name of Zach Tifton, called in sick the day of Roy's escape. Jackson is on his way to Tifton's apartment now. Maybe Tifton had been hiding Roy Carlton there at some point." Marsh shrugged. "Guess we don't have to worry about that issue now."

"We still need to know who helped Roy escape," Sam insisted. "In my opinion, both hospital employees, Zach Tifton and Cindy Gorlich, are still suspects. Either one or both could have been hired by the same person who shot and killed both Abbott and Carlton."

"You think they were taken out of commission by the same perp?" Marsh asked.

"I don't know for sure, but that's the way I'm leaning." He frowned. There were more holes in his theory than pieces of fabric holding it together. Yet his gut told him they were on the right track. "The timing of both murders, one right before Roy's escape and one a day after, is suspicious, don't you think?"

"Yeah, when you say it like that it's glaring. For sure the same person is behind this." Marsh paused, then added, "Or the same group of people are behind it."

The mere thought of a group of thugs being involved was depressing. But Marsh was right. They really had no idea what was behind all of this.

A motive strong enough to kill an innocent mother and her son.

He frowned when he realized Mari and Theo were shivering in the cold. "Let's get them into your SUV so they can warm up."

"Not a problem." Marsh turned and jogged over to start the SUV.

Sam moved closer to Mari. "You and Theo can sit inside the SUV for a few minutes, okay?"

"Thank you." Mari held the basket of eggs in one hand, ushering Theo forward with the other.

"How long until we can head back to the ranch house?"

"I'm not sure. We'll see what happens when the others arrive." He wasn't trying to be vague on purpose. Was it safe to return to the original ranch house? He knew Mari and Theo were more comfortable there, but he needed to make this decision based on facts, not to make Mari happy.

Once they were huddled in the back seat with the heat flowing through the vents, he headed back to the front of the ranch house. Examining the front porch, he frowned when he spotted a drop of blood.

"Marsh, over here." He gestured to the drop of blood. "Seems as if Roy was brought in this way."

"And where was the deputy while this was happening?" Marsh asked. "A bathroom break? Really?"

Sam turned to see two sheriff's department SUVs rolling up Mari's driveway. "Guess we'll find out."

"If we can trust them to tell the truth," Marsh muttered under his breath.

Sam silently agreed but kept his expression impassive as the two deputies emerged from their cars.

"You're Hayward, right?" the larger man asked. "We met the other day."

"Yes, I'm Texas Ranger Sam Hayward, and

this is Ranger Marshall Branson." He noticed neither deputy stepped forward to shake their hands. So that was how this was going to go. Adversaries rather than partners.

"We're Deputy Adam Grendel and Deputy Trey Drake." The four of them stood there with a good six feet between them. "What's this about a dead body being taken inside last night?"

Swallowing his irritation, he explained how he'd taken Mari and Theo to the original ranch house for safety, only to return this morning to find Carlton's dead body.

"The back door was open?" Grendel snorted. "That's probably how they got inside."

"There's blood on the front porch." Sam held the man's gaze. "Easy enough to have it tested to see if matches Carlton."

There was a long moment of silence as the two deputies digested that.

"I cleared the house, and it looks as if the bedrooms were tossed," Sam went on. "We know Jeff Abbott was killed down at Whistling Creek and left there, too. I'm no medical expert, but there's not nearly enough blood on the floor to indicate Carlton was killed inside. I believe he was dumped here as some sort of warning."

"What kind of warning?" Drake asked. "To you?"

He suppressed a sigh. "More likely a warning

for Ms. Lynch. She's been targeted several times now, starting back with an attempted abduction of her son."

"She knows something," Drake said, his expression suspicious. "We need to take her in for questioning."

Over his stone-cold dead body, Sam thought, but didn't say. "I've spoken to her at length. She has no idea why she's being targeted or how Roy Carlton escaped from prison. We need to figure out if Carlton was the shooter before he was killed, so I want his clothing and hands tested for gunshot residue."

"Sam is right. We've been working this case per the request of the governor," Marsh said. "We asked you to come out as a courtesy, since this transpired under your watch."

"This isn't our fault," Grendel snapped.

"You better watch it," Trey Drake added. "This is still our jurisdiction."

"No, it's not. I am putting you on notice that we'd like to interview the deputy who was assigned to watch the place. We're calling the shots from here on out."

Both deputies bristled at that, but thankfully the arrival of Tucker and Jackson prevented the tense situation from disintegrating into a full-blown shouting match.

Sam walked away, to keep himself from saying

something he might regret. He waited for Tuck and Jackson to join them.

"Medical examiner is on the way," Tucker said. "He's not happy about driving all this way out to the ranch for the second time in two days."

"Join the unhappy club." Marsh jerked his thumb toward the deputies. "Those guys are jerks."

"Nothing new there," Jackson said. "We got similar attitude when asking about Deputy Erickson, the guy who was supposed to be guarding Carlton prior to his escape."

"Where are Mari and Theo?" Tucker asked.

"In the SUV, keeping warm." He hesitated, then said, "All was quiet last night down at the original ranch house, but I'm having doubts about staying there indefinitely. Especially after this latest incident."

His fellow rangers were quiet for a long moment. "The fact that Carlton's body was dumped here is concerning. But if no one has been around the original ranch house, it should be safe enough," Jackson finally said. "Especially with one of us standing guard."

One of *them*—not Sam—was the not-so-subtle distinction. And Sam understood Jackson's concern. Every cell in his body rejected the idea of leaving Mari and Theo with someone else watching over them, but he managed to nod in agreement. "Whatever you think is best. But I am worried that this killer is escalating. If I were involved in this scheme, whatever it is, I would be concerned that I'd be targeted next."

The rangers exchanged a look. "Maybe we need to get that message out to our two hospital employee suspects," Tucker drawled. "That might encourage them to cooperate with us."

"If they're guilty, yeah," Marsh agreed. "But for all we know, there was someone else involved."

"I know you've questioned Mari," Jackson said. "But there must be something we're missing. Some key reason why this guy is coming after her."

"I'm open to suggestions," Sam said, doing his best not to show his frustration. "And frankly, Mari is, too. She has expressed her concerns about why this is happening several times. If she knew anything, she would tell us to protect her son."

Another long silence hung between them.

This time, the arrival of the medical examiner ended the conversation. Dr. Earl Bond slid out from behind the wheel, approaching them with his field kit.

"You guys need to figure out what's going on," he grumbled. "This is getting ridiculous."

"We're doing our best. This way." Sam turned

to take the lead. He paused on the front porch, pointing out the drop of blood. "What do you think, Doc? Could this be from our victim?"

"Get your crime scene techs here to take a sample and I'll let you know." Despite his annoyance at the long drive, Earl Bond looked around with interest as Sam took him inside the house.

"I didn't touch him," Sam said. "Based on the stench and the bullet hole in his head, there was no reason to get close. I believe he's been gone for at least a couple of hours."

Dr. Earl Bond grunted and went to work, donning booties, a white coverall, mask and gloves. He knelt beside the body and went to work.

"One more thing, Doc," Sam said, breathing carefully through his mouth to avoid the worst of the smell. "We would like his hands bagged for gunpowder residue. And his clothing preserved, too."

"That's not a problem." Dr. Bond quickly placed two paper bags over Carlton's hands and taped them around the wrist to keep them in place. "The sooner your crime scene techs get out here, the better. Gunpowder residue can dissipate over time."

"I'll check to see how far out they are." Gratefully, he stepped back outside. Then frowned, when he saw Marshall getting in behind the wheel of his SUV. "Where's Marsh going?"

Tucker arched a brow. "He's taking Mari and Theo back to the original ranch house using the SUV instead of the four-wheeler. Why?"

"No reason. I'm glad they're going back to where it's safe." At least, that was what he said out loud.

But deep down, he was irked that Marsh had made that decision without telling him.

Then he realized the three rangers had likely discussed it among themselves, making the decision while Sam was busy inside.

Leaving him little choice but to go along with the plan.

TEN

"Where is Sam?" Mari eyed Marshall with confusion. "Isn't he coming with us?"

"He'll meet up with us later." Marshall slid behind the wheel. "I'm hoping you know a way we can get across to your grandfather's ranch house without wrecking the SUV."

"I—uh, sure." Swallowing a protest, she began giving directions. The old driveway was little more than a dirt road, and they had to cross the pasture to the west to get to it. As the SUV bumped and swayed over the uneven ground, she gave Theo's hand a reassuring squeeze. The poor kid had been through a lot and was handling it better than she could have hoped.

She kept the basket of eggs in her lap. Not exactly the food supplies she'd hoped for, but better than nothing.

"I want my trucks," Theo whined. "How come we didn't get my trucks?"

"I'll see if Mr. Sam can bring them later." She

caught Marshall's keen gaze on her in the rearview mirror. "If not, we'll play with your horses again. This is Mr. Marshall. Can you say hi?"

"Hi," Theo mumbled, hiding his face against Charlie.

Marshall's eyes darted to Theo for a moment, before looking out at the dirt road. She wondered if he had a child of his own or was baffled at how kids behaved. Being a single parent wasn't easy. Kids needed constant attention and room to run and play. Which normally wasn't a problem living out on Whistling Creek Ranch.

Unfortunately, the only outdoor activity Theo had experienced lately was building their minisnowman. She told herself not to dwell on what she wasn't able to provide Theo. Best to focus on the positive side of their situation.

Thanks to God's grace and the Texas Rangers, they were alive and unharmed. And Roy was dead. He would never hurt her or Theo again.

The nagging thought about why she and Theo had been targeted wouldn't leave her alone. Roy must have told someone about her, making them believe that she knew details of the crime. Or maybe Roy had bragged about how much her ranch was worth.

She almost wished the killer would simply come up and talk to her so she could reassure him that she knew nothing and had very little cash. Maybe then they would leave her alone.

Talk about wishful thinking. She gave herself a mental shake. There was no point in speculating. She needed to trust in God's plan.

And in Sam and his fellow rangers' ability to get to the bottom of this mess.

"That's the house up ahead," she said, leaning forward in her seat. "Do you see it?"

"Yep." Marshall seemed like a nice enough guy. She didn't doubt that he'd protect her and Theo.

But she missed Sam. Which was ridiculous since she barely knew him.

Marshall pulled up to the front of the house. It looked unchanged since they'd left it—what, not even two hours ago? So much had happened, it seemed longer. She helped Theo out of the SUV, then grabbed her basket of eggs. Holding Theo's hand, she followed Marshall inside.

There was a chill in the air, and Marshall didn't hesitate to cross over to add more wood to the stove. She set the basket of eggs on the counter and quickly washed them.

"I want my trucks," Theo repeated, this time stamping his foot for emphasis. It would have been cute if not for her frayed nerves.

"Can you tell me about your horses?" Marshall asked.

She flashed him a grateful look.

Theo eagerly played with Marshall and his horses, reinforcing the little boy's need for a father figure. Not that Sam, Marshall or any of the others were volunteering for the job.

Well, they were stepping up to help now, but only on a temporary basis. And she was truly grateful for their kind and seemingly endless patience.

Playtime came to an end, though, when Marshall's phone rang. She watched as he rose to his feet and pulled out his phone.

"Branson," he answered curtly.

There was a long pause as Marshall listened to whatever the caller was telling him. She couldn't help watching him curiously, but his impassive gaze didn't reveal any indication of a change in the case.

Not good news, then, she thought with a sigh. Of course it couldn't be that easy.

"Okay, I'll let the guys know. Someone will head in to interview him again."

"Interview who?" she asked after he'd slipped his phone back into his pocket.

Marshall slowly nodded. "A suspect we believe may have been seen riding in the blue van with your ex-husband."

"His possible girlfriend, Cindy Gorlich?" she

guessed. "She's the one who reported her van was stolen, right?"

"No. The other hospital employee, Zach Tifton." Marshall grimaced. "The witness description was vague, but we haven't found Zach yet to interview him. He never answered his door yesterday and we couldn't see anything suspicious through the windows. Without a search warrant or probable cause, we couldn't enter the premises. With this added information of a witness describing him as possibly with Carlton, we'll get what we need to do the search."

She understood the laws were there to protect the innocent, yet still felt irritated at how Marshall and the other rangers had their hands tied while trying to find out who was responsible for the attempted kidnapping of Theo and shooting at her.

"I'm glad." It was something, a step in the right direction. Even if it seemed like things were moving in slow motion.

"Roy never mentioned seeing anyone?" Marshall asked.

She swallowed a sigh. "Sam already asked me this. No, I was not aware of any girlfriend. And wouldn't have cared, even if I had known about it."

"Sorry, we're still trying to put the puzzle pieces together," he said with a chagrined smile.

"We know Carlton killed Hank George, but there's obviously something more going on here than a simple murder."

"Yes." A strange thought struck. "What if Roy didn't murder Hank George?"

Marshall frowned. "We know he did. His fingerprints were on the gun, his DNA at the scene of the crime."

She nodded. "Yes, you're right. There was a lot of evidence against him. When you guys were talking about the deputies not doing a good job, I couldn't help but wonder if the fingerprints, gun and DNA were planted there to implicate him." She flushed. "Or maybe I just watch too many crime shows."

Marshall smiled, but then his gaze turned thoughtful. "That is an angle we hadn't considered. Although I would think that Carlton would have cried foul to anyone who would listen about being framed."

"You would think so." She shook her head. "Don't mind me. It's been a long couple of days."

"I understand." Marshall's gaze was sympathetic. He glanced around the room. "I'll bring in more wood," he offered.

"Sam stacked a bunch of wood just outside the back door, so no need. We'll be fine."

"Mr. Marshall do you want to see my snowman?" Theo asked.

"Ah, sure." Marshall glanced at her as if for approval. She nodded, and quickly put Theo's coat, hat, boots and mitten back on before following the pair to the back door.

She stayed inside, watching as Theo ran toward the mini-snowman they'd made. It was already beginning to melt thanks to the bright sunlight.

She was about to turn away to begin lunch, when the sound of gunfire sent her heart to her throat.

Theo! Yanking the door open, she rushed outside in time to see Marshall scoop Theo into his arms, bolting toward her.

"Get inside, hurry!"

She turned and darted back inside, holding the door open for Marshall and Theo.

"Get down, stay away from the windows," Marshall said as he put Theo in her arms, pulled his phone and called Sam for backup. "Sam? Gunfire at the original ranch house. I need you guys here right away!"

Theo sobbed as she held him close. She was thankful her son wasn't hurt but was equally horrified to know the gunman had found them here, at her grandfather's original ranch house.

Almost as if he'd been sitting out there and waiting for the right time to strike.

She fought the urge to cry, sick with the realization they weren't safe, anywhere.

* * *

The call from Marsh about gunfire at the ranch house made Sam wish for the tenth time that he was the one out there with Mari and Theo.

"Tuck, you and Jackson take the SUV. I'm going on the four-wheeler." He didn't waste another second in running to jump onto the four-wheeler. The all-terrain vehicle could get him there faster than using an alternate route.

At least, that was what he hoped. Especially since he knew exactly where to go.

He never should have left them alone. And he also shouldn't have assumed the original ranch house was safe.

They couldn't stay at Whistling Creek any longer. Mari wouldn't like it, but there wasn't another alternative.

Not after this.

He drove as quickly as he dared, not wanting to flip the machine, but desperate to make good time. When the ranch house came into view, he didn't slow down as he raked his gaze over the area.

Marsh's SUV was parked out front and appeared undamaged. He hadn't wasted time in getting details from Marsh as to where the shots had come from and knew the shooter had been stationed out back.

And could be making his way up to the house right now.

Gunning the engine, Sam drove around the corner of the house. Scanning the trees, he searched for signs of a shooter with a rifle and scope, much like the guy who'd taken up residence outside Mari's house when he'd shot through her living room window.

He didn't see anything, but that didn't mean much. What he did notice was a bullet hole in the mini-snowman he, Mari and Theo had built yesterday.

He kept moving, doing his best to draw the gunman's fire. But to no avail.

After rounding the next corner of the house, he went back to where Marsh's SUV was parked. Killing the engine of the ATV, he jumped off and ran up to the front door.

"Mari? Marsh? Are you okay?"

The door opened, revealing a grim-faced Marsh. "No one is hurt. But we need to get out of here."

"I know." He stepped inside, his chest tightening when he saw Mari and Theo sitting on the floor, tucked behind the wood-burning stove.

With the cast-iron stove as protection, it was probably the safest spot in the house.

"Are you sure you're both okay?" He couldn't help but cross the room to kneel beside them.

Mari sniffled, her eyes red and puffy from crying. "We're not hurt."

He put a hand on Theo's back, wishing more than anything he could do more for them. Then he stood and turned to face Marsh. "Did you get a line on the shooter?"

"He was directly across from the back door," Marsh said. "I noticed the flash of his scope a second before he fired. Thankfully, I was already grabbing Theo and turning to head inside."

He wanted to thank Marsh for saving their lives but knew that was their job. His fault that he cared more for Theo and Mari than he should.

"Tuck and Jackson are bringing the other SUV," he explained. "Looks like yours isn't damaged, which is good. We should all drive out together, keeping Theo and Mari in the front vehicle and the other covering from behind."

"You're assuming the shooter hasn't already made his way around to the front to lie in wait for us," Marsh said. "I've been checking every window, but just because I haven't seen him doesn't mean he's not out there. There's a lot of land to use as cover."

That was true. Sam knew he couldn't afford to make another mistake. "Okay, then what's the plan?"

There was a long moment of silence before Marsh said, "We don't have another option. We'll drive out while keeping Mari and Theo covered.

Even if this guy does try to take another shot, he'll have to go through us to get to them."

Since he couldn't come up with anything different, he nodded. "Okay. Tuck and Jackson should be here soon."

"Where are we going?" Mari asked. "I mean, once we leave here."

He hadn't given their destination much thought. Other than getting them away from the shooter. If he had his way, he'd stick her in a plane and send her and Theo to another state, far away from the ranch.

But that wasn't a feasible option. Rangers only had jurisdiction in the state of Texas, and they needed to be close enough to continue working the case.

"We'll find a motel," he finally said. "At least we'll have easy access to food."

"Are you going to tell the deputies where we're going?" she pressed.

"No." He glanced at Marsh, who nodded his agreement. "Only the four of us rangers will know your location."

She nodded and pressed a kiss to Theo's head. "Okay. But I'll need to make sure Tom Fleming can continue helping with the ranch chores."

"Call him now," Sam suggested. He glanced at his watch. "We have a few minutes before Tucker and Jackson will be here."

She scooted out from behind the wood-burning stove, her face flushed from the heat. Without thinking about it, Sam reached to take Theo into his arms. The little boy wound his arms around Sam's neck and buried his face against his chest.

"I'm scared," Theo whispered.

Sam's heart squeezed in his chest. No child should be in this position. "It's okay, I'm here. We're all safe now." He did his best to sound reassuring.

Marsh raked his hand through his hair. "Maybe I should have scouted the place."

"Even if you had, finding a guy hiding in the woods wouldn't be easy." He cleared his throat as Theo continued to cling to him. It hurt to know how frightened he was. "It's my fault for suggesting we continue using this place. I should have known it was only a matter of time before the perp showed up."

Marsh nodded, and they were both quiet while Mari spoke with Tom Fleming, her closest neighbor.

"I'm sorry to do this to you and Irene," she said. "I feel terrible asking for favors." There was a pause as she listened, before she said, "Yes, I know. And I appreciate that. Thanks again, Tom." She lowered her phone and turned to face him. "I feel awful. Tom has his own ranch chores, too. I really can't impose on him for long."

"I know." He felt bad for her plight. The sound of a car engine had him heading toward the front window. "Tuck and Jackson are here."

"Good." Marsh joined him at the window.

Without being asked, Tuck parked the SUV right next to the other one, leaving just a few feet between them. Tuck and Jackson slid out and glanced around before stepping up to the front door.

Marsh was there to let them in.

Sam quickly outlined his plan. "We don't know the shooter's location. He may have taken off because he missed or he's waiting up ahead somewhere along the dirt road to take another shot."

"I doubt he's gone," Tuck muttered. "Seems like he wouldn't come this far not to finish the job."

Mari's face paled, making Sam wince. They were used to talking about this stuff, but it was different to be the intended victim.

"I want Marsh to drive the first SUV. Tuck, you take the second. I'll stay in the back seat of Marsh's car with Mari and Theo hiding in the back seat. Jackson, you ride with Tuck, but in the back seat as if you're protecting them, too." He shrugged. "The shooter will hopefully assume we have them in the second vehicle, not the first. It's not much of a decoy operation, but it's all I have."

"That works," Jackson agreed. "Especially if you make sure they both stay out of sight."

"That's the plan." He glanced around. "Ready?"

"I hav'ta go to the bathroom," Theo said, lifting his head from Sam's chest.

"I can take him." Mari stepped forward.

"We'll both take him." From this point forward, Sam wasn't going to let Mari and Theo out of his sight.

He couldn't help feeling responsible for this most recent incident. Even though he knew Marsh had done everything right.

The trip to the bathroom didn't take too long. Theo wanted his stuffed dog and his horses, so Mari bundled them into a small blanket in lieu of a bag.

"He deserves to have something familiar with him," she said in a low voice.

"I agree." Sam put his hand in the center of her back. "We're going to move quickly once we're outside, okay? Just get into the back seat and I'll hand you Theo, and crawl in beside you. Make sure to get down on the floor."

She nodded in understanding and shrugged into her coat. As always it took another moment or two to get Theo bundled up, but apparently sensing the seriousness of the situation, the little boy didn't argue.

Marsh stepped out first, with Mari right behind him. Within minutes, Mari and Theo were down on the floor, with Sam hovering nearby.

Marsh pulled away from the ranch house first. Sam glanced through the rearview mirror to see that Tuck was driving the second SUV, with Jackson positioned in the back, pretending to cover two people just like Sam was.

This would work. It had to.

Marsh kept his speed steady, not too fast over the rocky terrain but not too slow either. Sam scanned both sides of the dirt road but didn't see anyone.

They were roughly past the halfway point, taking a curve in the road when the crack of gunfire rang out.

Marsh hit the gas, and so did Tuck. Sam hunched over Mari and Theo, knowing there was little they could do but to keep going.

And pray.

ELEVEN

Another gunshot rang out. Mari flinched at the sound, even though she didn't think their vehicle was hit.

At least, not yet.

Hearing Sam's whispered prayers for safety helped keep her calm. She hadn't expected the shooter to be waiting for them, but it was clear Sam had. He'd planned for the worst, and she mentally braced herself for what would happen if their vehicle was struck and disabled by a bullet.

She had faith in Sam, Marshall, Tucker and Jackson's ability to get them out of this mess. But she was upset by the constant danger. Roy was dead. Why were they still coming after her and Theo?

What on earth did they want?

"Tuck's SUV took a round," Marshall said. "They're still moving, but slower now. The gap between us is widening."

"We can't leave them behind," Sam said.

"Tuck is waving at us to keep going," Marshall responded calmly. "He and Jackson can take care of themselves."

Sam's jaw clenched, but then he looked down at her and Theo with a resigned gaze. She felt terrible for making him choose between backing up his team and protecting them.

"I'll call to get the deputies out here," Sam said after a long moment. He swayed from side to side as Marshall picked up the pace, while pulling his phone from his pocket. "They need to offer assistance to Tuck and Jackson."

"Good idea." Marshall was preoccupied with driving while she listened as Sam made the call.

The gunfire had stopped now, making her wonder if the shooter believed she and Theo were hiding in the second car. She sent up a silent prayer for the rangers' safety.

Please, Lord Jesus, keep those brave men safe in Your care!

"Now!" Sam barked into his phone. "They're taking gunfire, understand? They need you now."

She held Theo's hand and lightly stroked his hair. He clutched Charlie close, but wasn't crying. As awful as it was, she suspected her son was becoming accustomed to the sound of gunfire.

No child should be put in this position. What had Roy gotten himself involved with? Who had killed him? And why?

She had no answers, only dozens of unan-
swered questions.

Marshall must be closer to the road now, because she heard the wail of sirens. Her heart
squeezed at knowing they'd left Tucker and Jackson behind.

"I'm sure the shooter will take off," Marshall
said.

Sam nodded, but then dug for his phone again.
A minute later, he said, "Tuck? Are you both
okay? Where's the shooter?"

"We're fine." She was so close to Sam she could
hear both sides of the conversation. "He hit our
engine block, though, so we had to stop and get
out of the car. We returned fire, but didn't get a
good look at him."

She swallowed hard, imagining the two rangers exchanging gunfire with someone who'd tried
to kill her and Theo.

"Deputies are on the way," Sam was saying.
"Hitch a ride with them. We'll catch up with you,
later."

"Roger that," Tucker said before ending the
call.

"I'm so glad they're both unharmed," she whispered. "That was close."

"Too close, but thankfully our plan worked. He
shot at both of us, but only took out one of the
vehicles. The wrong one," he added.

But it could have gone the other way. She could tell by Sam's grim expression that he'd feared they'd all perish in the most recent shooting event.

And they could have.

God was watching over them. And knowing that gave her the inner strength she needed to keep going.

The sirens from the sheriff's department vehicles were louder now. She couldn't see, but Sam's gaze tracked the cars, so she could imagine them going around their SUV to reach the dirt road driveway.

"Can we trust them?" she asked.

"The call went out on the radio to dispatch, so yeah. I don't think they'll pull anything now." Sam looked at her. "How are you holding up?"

"My legs are starting to cramp," she admitted. Being down in a crouch like this wasn't normal.

"Marsh? Are we far enough that they can get up on the car seats?"

"Give me a couple minutes. I'm almost at the point where I can get off this road and onto the main highway."

"I can wait." She shifted a bit. Her main concern was Theo's safety. They didn't have a car seat for him.

The minutes passed slowly. Finally, Sam said, "Okay, you can get up now."

He leaned back and she slowly straightened into a normal sitting position. She stretched her legs out as far as possible to relieve the pressure. Then she reached for Theo.

"We need to stop and get a car seat for him," she said as she buckled him into the middle space between her and Sam.

Marshall met her gaze in the rearview. "We'll stop when we get closer to Austin."

Austin? She frowned. "Why there?"

"There are more hotel options," Sam said. "Especially on the outskirts of town. And that is the city where the original murder took place of City Manager Hank George." He frowned. "We need to be close enough to continue following up on leads in the investigation."

"Okay." Easy enough to accept that rationale. The sooner they figured out what was going on, the quicker she and Theo could return home.

To their normal, boring and safe life.

It would seem different after spending so much time with Sam and the other rangers. But she quickly pushed that thought aside. She would take the mundane routine over being in constant danger, any day.

Yet that didn't mean she wouldn't miss Sam.

He's not yours to care about. She gave herself a mental shake. There was no point in wishing for something she couldn't have. Even if Sam was interested, any sort of relationship between them would be impossible. She lived and worked on the ranch. Texas Rangers were sent to work cases all over the state.

And besides, she doubted Sam would want anything to do with a ready-made family.

Unfortunately, memories of his warm kiss wouldn't leave her alone. Logically, she knew she was in a vulnerable position. Her life and Theo's depended on Sam and the others.

Marshall, Tucker and Jackson were all nice, brave and good-looking men. But she wasn't attracted to them.

Not in the way she was so keenly aware of Sam.

"Should we stop at the shopping center?" Sam's question interrupted her tumultuous thoughts.

She glanced over to the discount shopping store. "That would be great. Thank you."

"No problem." Marsh met her gaze briefly in the rearview mirror. She hoped her thoughts about Sam hadn't been obvious to him. "I'll wait for you in the car. That way, I can drop you off near the front door and pick you up, there, too."

"Works for me," Sam agreed.

"That would be wonderful." She was grateful for the opportunity to get Theo a proper car seat, and maybe a couple more toys to keep him occupied. It was bad enough to know her son was in danger; she needed to keep him calm and happy.

"Wait a minute," Sam warned as Marshall pulled up to the front door. She unbelted Theo as Sam ran around to open her door. He was on high alert as they slid out of the SUV and headed inside.

It felt odd to do something as normal as shopping thirty minutes after nearly being struck by gunfire. The good news was that there were plenty of after-Christmas sales on toys. The car seat wasn't cheap, but she was able to find some action figures marked half off.

"Would you like a change of clothes for you and Theo, too?" Sam asked. He didn't appear concerned at how quickly their cart was filling up. "Grab what you need since I'm not sure how long we'll be staying in the hotel."

"Okay."

"Will we be home for my birthday?" Theo asked. "And how will Billy the elf know that I'm being good while we're at the hotel?"

"I—uh, don't know." His questions had caught her off guard.

"When is your birthday, Theo?" Sam asked.

Theo held up two fingers. Sam frowned. "You're not two years old, you're going to be five, aren't you?"

"No, my birthday is two," he insisted. "Day two."

"January second," she clarified. "We call it day two of the new year."

"Oh, I see. Of course. Day two." Sam nodded as if the explanation made perfect sense. "Well, Theo, I'm going to do everything I can to make sure you're home by your birthday."

"Goody," Theo clapped his hands excitedly. "I want to open more presents."

She suppressed a sigh. She didn't like that he was all about the gifts, but knew most kids were. And for Theo, Christmas overshadowed his birthday.

She tried to make it a special day, but based on what they were going through now, it would be more than enough to have the shooter arrested and the danger over, for good.

Walking through the store, easing past other shoppers searching for a discount in the after-holiday sale, he thought about Theo's upcoming birthday.

He didn't like making promises he may not be able to keep. Telling the boy that he'd have him home by his birthday wasn't smart. Yet the kid had been through a lot and deserved something positive to look forward to.

The little boy's birthday was four days away. Surely they'd have the gunman in custody by then.

Although Roy Carlton's murder had brought

their investigation to a grinding halt. Or rather, the murder had forced them to take a sharp detour from their original theory to something more complicated.

He still didn't trust the sheriff's department.

"No more," Mari scolded her son. "You have enough toys."

Sam wanted to let the kid have whatever he wanted but knew better than to interfere. He stopped in the electronics section to pick up a cheap laptop, hoping to get more work done while they were hiding out at the hotel.

When they went through the checkout, Mari's eyes widened in horror at the amount.

"We can get rid of some of this," she said, grabbing at some items. "We don't need it all."

"It's fine." He rested his hand on her arm. "Please, Mari. I don't mind. It's the least I can do. Besides, the bulk of the cost is the computer, followed by the car seat. And that's a necessity. The rest isn't that much."

She gazed up at him for a long moment, before acquiescing. "You shouldn't have to pay for this—my situation isn't your fault," she protested weakly.

"Or yours," he pointed out. "As far as the toys go, consider them an early birthday present for Theo."

She nodded, but still looked concerned as he

handed over his credit card. He admired her desire to stay independent, but these were extraneous circumstances.

And he knew her inability to work the ranch would put them in a hole, financially.

Before heading outside, he called Marsh. "We're ready."

"Be there in two."

As promised, Marsh pulled up to the main doors. Sam stored the bag of clothing and toys in the back, leaving Mari to secure Theo's car seat. The little boy protested having to climb inside, but Mari was firm.

"Now. Or no toys."

The boy glanced at Sam, then did his mother's bidding. Sam could only imagine how difficult it must be for Mari to be a single mother, dealing with Theo every day.

Not an easy job, especially while running a ranch.

Once they were settled at chain motel, Sam reached out to Tucker. "Where are you?"

"Heading to Austin." Sam could hear talking in the background. "Deputy Grendel has agreed to take us to get a rental SUV."

"No sign of the shooter, then?"

"Knowing he was armed and dangerous, we didn't stick around," Tucker admitted. "But the plan is to head back later to look for shell casings."

"Understood." Shell casings would be nice, especially if they matched those found beneath the tree outside the front of Mari's ranch house. But that wasn't worth risking their lives either. He gave Tucker the name of their motel. "We have a pair of connecting rooms. Meet us here when you're finished. We need to follow up on our next move."

"Got it. Later." Tucker ended the call.

"Are you leaving us here alone?" Mari asked, her gaze troubled.

"No." He crossed over to where she sat on the edge of the bed. Theo was thankfully distracted by his new toys, especially the action figures and the cartoons on the television. He sank beside her. "One of us will always be with you and Theo."

She nodded, dropping her gaze to her entwined hands. He slipped his arm around her shoulders, giving her a reassuring hug.

"I'm sorry," he murmured. "I wish there was more for me to do to make you and Theo feel safe."

"We are safe with you." She glanced up at him, her green eyes direct. "I can't tell you how happy I am that God brought you to the ranch house when we needed you the most."

He was touched by her comment, and smiled at how she'd met him with the business end of a shotgun. "Me, too."

She leaned against him. He wanted very badly

to kiss her again, but couldn't bring himself to do that in front of Theo.

"Sam?" Marsh hovered in the opening between their connecting rooms. His arched eyebrow seemed to indicate he could read Sam's thoughts. "Owens wants to chat with us."

"Yeah." He forced himself to release Mari. "I'm coming."

Was it his imagination or did Mari's fingers linger on his arm before he moved across the room. He glanced over his shoulder to find her watching him. It was all he could do not to turn and go back to her side.

He wasn't sure why he felt so deeply connected to her. He should have learned his lesson after last time.

But here he was, about to make the same mistake all over again. Okay, he knew Mari wasn't anything like Leanne. She wasn't a criminal or involved in this mess.

Yet getting emotionally involved wasn't smart.

"Skating on thin ice," Marsh murmured as he joined him in the next room. "Better watch out that you don't fall through and drown."

"Yeah, yeah." He wasn't in the mood to discuss his complicated feelings for Mari and Theo.

Or maybe the problem was they weren't all that complicated. He liked her. Respected her. Admired her. And cared about them both.

More than he should.

Marsh sighed, then pulled out his phone. A moment later he had their boss on the line.

"Where have you been?" Captain John Owens didn't sound happy. "The trail is going cold."

"Sorry Cap," Marsh said. "We experienced more gunfire getting the two targets away from Whistling Creek Ranch."

"Gunfire? Anyone hurt?" Owens asked.

"No injuries, but we're down another SUV," Sam said.

"Our budget is spiraling out of control on this case," Owens muttered. "Did you get the shooter?"

"No." Marsh winced at admitting the failure. "The good news is that we have the targets safe just outside of Austin."

"I'm getting a lot of heat from the chief on this," Owens said in a blunt tone. "First a prisoner escapes, then he's found dead. And we have squat to go on."

"Any updates from the crime scene techs?" Sam asked, more to distract their boss from the lack of progress. "And what about getting those search warrants for Cindy Gorlich and Zach Tifton?"

"I have the search warrant for Tifton here. I just need one of you guys to head out to execute it." Owens still sounded testy. "I'm working on getting search warrants for Gorlich, too."

"I'll grab and execute the warrant for Tifton," Marsh offered. Sam felt a little guilty letting Marsh do the legwork while he stayed here with Mari and Theo. "Tuck and Jackson will be here soon. I'll grab one of them to go with me."

"Good. I'll keep working on the warrant for Gorlich, although the judge is making noises that we don't have enough evidence against her. The witness seeing a man matching Tifton's description was enough for us to get that warrant."

"I picked up a computer today, so I'll dig into Gorlich's social media," he offered. "If we can find some connection between her and Roy Carlton, the judge should grant the warrant."

"Do it," Owens said. "I need something for the upper brass, soon."

"We should know soon about whether or not Roy Carlton has gunshot residue on his hands or chest, too," Sam said. "I asked the medical examiner to protect both areas."

"That would be nice," Owens said. "Get back to me ASAP."

"Understood. We'll be in touch." Marsh quickly ended the call, shaking his head with a grimace. "He's right, we should have more intel by now."

"I know." Sam crossed to the desk where he'd left the laptop. "I'll start on this end right away."

"I'll head out to the office," Marsh said. Their headquarters were in Austin, which was another reason staying in a motel here was better for all of them.

Leaving Mari and Theo alone in the other room wasn't easy, but he forced himself to concentrate on the task at hand. Yet digging into Cindy Gorlich's social media didn't reveal any connection to Roy Carlton.

Was it a coincidence that her van was stolen? Maybe since it was a make and model known to be easier to steal than most.

He decided to search for a connection between Cindy and Zach but was quickly interrupted by a phone call from Tucker.

"We're five minutes away," Tuck said.

"You should head out to back up Marsh. He's executing a search warrant for Zach Tifton's place," he said. "We're fine here."

"Sounds good. We'll talk more later."

Sam lowered his phone, feeling guilty all over again for sitting here while the others did the legwork on the investigation.

Giving up on social media, he used a simple case search to dig into Cindy's past. Almost immediately, he reached for his phone.

"Tuck? Cindy Gorlich has several open financial cases against her, including a pending eviction from her apartment." He rose to his feet. "She needs money. Get over to headquarters.

This may be enough to get a search warrant for her, too."

"Roger that. We're on our way."

Sam ended the call, then contacted Owens, convinced they were on to something. Anyone suffering a financial crisis could be swayed into doing something crazy.

Like helping Roy Carlton break out of the hospital.

TWELVE

Hovering in the doorway between their connecting rooms, Mari overheard Sam's comment about Cindy Gorlich having financial trouble.

"Does this mean Roy wasn't having an affair with Cindy?" She asked.

Sam swung around to face her. "That may have been the wrong assumption," he admitted. "It's looking more like she may have been paid to help your ex-husband escape."

She nodded, wondering why that made her feel better. It wasn't as if she still loved Roy. Not just because of the way he'd verbally and then physically abused her, but he'd killed Hank George in cold blood.

She hadn't known the man she'd married. And he'd only pretended to care about her. Why he'd bothered to marry her in the first place, she had no idea. Unless he'd wanted to look like a legitimate family man.

Whatever. That was in the past. No point in

playing the what-if game. Besides, she firmly believed God's plan was to give her the blessing of a son.

"We plan to search both Cindy's apartment and Zach Tifton's place." Sam's voice intruded on her thoughts. A flash of anticipation lightened his dark brown eyes. "Hopefully we'll find key evidence that will help us find out who hired them."

"I hope so, too." She glanced back over her shoulder to make sure Theo was still watching cartoons. The motel offered a channel featuring children's movies, and Theo was thrilled to have extra television time. "I need to call Tom Fleming. Do you have any idea how long we'll be here?"

"No, sorry." Sam gave her an apologetic glance. "I wish I could say we'll have this wrapped up by tomorrow, but it's better if we take it day by day."

She understood where he was coming from. She tried not to sigh as she reached for her phone to make the call. Tom was nice enough about the inconvenience, and she made a silent promise to make it up to Tom and Irene later, bringing them eggs and maybe some steaks from her last butchering along with fresh bread.

"Everything okay?" Sam asked.

"Yes." She knew Tom would only gather eggs twice a day, rather than her usual three times in the winter months, but that couldn't be helped. "Is there something I can do?"

"I'm afraid not." Sam held her gaze for a moment, then seemed to change his mind. "Can you fill me in on what you remember about your ex-husband's activities prior to your divorce? Any unusual behavior? Or maybe places that he went that were outside the norm?"

She checked Theo one more time, smiling at the picture he made curled up on the bed with Charlie, before stepping into the room. "I didn't know anything about Roy's plan to murder Hank George. To be honest, once I left him to go back to the ranch with Theo, I refused to communicate with him directly. My dad helped me get a lawyer to first file for separation and then divorce. From that point on, I referred Roy to Larry Eastman for everything."

Sam nodded. "Okay, but what about prior to that? You said he grew more abusive, first verbally, then physically. Was there anything you noticed prior to the change? I recall Roy worked in construction."

She sat on the edge of the bed, thinking back to those difficult years. "Yes, he did work in construction. He was good at doing drywall, referring to himself as a rocker." She shrugged. "Whatever that means. There were many new homes going up in the Austin suburbs at the time.

I do remember something about how Longhorn Construction, the company he worked for, had lost a key contract. I didn't think much about it at the time, but that may have been when he started drinking more." She stared down at her hands for a moment. "I soon learned to stay away from him when he'd been drinking, because he turned mean and nasty."

"I'm sorry you had to go through that," Sam said, coming over to sit beside her. "Did you get the impression he needed money?"

She frowned. "Not that I was aware of. But honestly, he handled all the bills. When I left that night with Theo, I only took our clothes and my car. Nothing else, even though I worked as a substitute teacher and had money in our joint checking account.

A flash of anger darkened his eyes. "That's not right. I hope you got some of that money back after the divorce."

"No, I didn't, because the money was gone." She remembered how awful she felt leaning on her father for financial support. "I didn't care, I was just so happy to be away from him. Then Roy was arrested for murder, and well, you know the rest."

"Yeah. So, other than the lost building contract you don't remember anything else."

"No. I wish I did." She grimaced. "What I regret the most was giving up my full-time teaching job. I should never have allowed Roy to have that much power over me." Looking back, it was glaringly easy to see her mistakes. Too bad she hadn't been smart enough to avoid some of them.

"Will you go back to teaching once Theo is in school?" Sam asked.

"Maybe." She had considered it. "Running the ranch takes a lot of time and energy, but more so during the spring, summer and fall. I've thought about doing substitute teaching work, especially in the winter. It would pay better than my egg money," she added with a smile.

He frowned. "I don't like knowing you're having trouble making ends meet."

"We're doing okay. We're blessed to have a roof over our heads and food to eat. That's more than some people have."

"True." He slipped his arm around her shoulders. The urge to lean against him was strong. "You're an amazing woman, Mari."

His kind words brought tears to her eyes. She blinked them back, reminding herself that he was just being nice because of her situation.

She managed a smile. "Thank you. You're pretty wonderful yourself."

"Ah, Mari," he murmured, hugging her close.

His musky scent filled her head, making her long for more. She gave in to temptation, resting her head in the hollow of his shoulder. On some level she wished she could stay in his arms like this, forever.

He brushed a sweet kiss against her temple. The gesture only increased her awareness of him. She lifted her head to look up at him, at the same moment he lowered his mouth to hers.

Their second kiss was even more powerful than the first. Slipping her arm around his waist, she pulled him closer. Sitting on the side of the bed was awkward, but she didn't move, didn't dare break off their embrace.

Because she wanted this, too much.

"Mommy!" Theo's cry was like a bucket of cold water sluicing over her head. She jerked away from Sam, jumping guiltily to her feet.

"I'm here, Theo." She hurried through the connecting door, to find Theo rubbing his eyes with his fists. Had he fallen asleep? "What's wrong?"

"The scary man," he whispered, clutching Charlie. "I saw him."

A chill snaked down her spine and she glanced at the window overlooking the parking lot. Then she relaxed, realizing Theo must have had a nightmare. "It's okay, sweetie. We're safe here. Mr. Sam will protect us."

As if on cue, Sam came over join them. "Hey, Theo." He rested a hand on her son's head. "Don't worry, I looked outside. No one is out there."

"'Kay," Theo mumbled. Her son rested against her. "I don't want the scary man to come back."

"I know, and Mr. Sam is here to make sure that doesn't happen." She met Sam's gaze, surprised to realize there was a hint of self-reproach in his gaze.

Sam obviously regretted their kiss. Swallowing hard, she looked away, stroking a hand down Theo's back.

Of course Sam wasn't interested in her that way. And she understood that most men weren't jumping at the chance to have a ready-made family.

She needed to remember this situation was temporary. That Sam was only there to keep them safe.

Tearing himself away from Mari and Theo wasn't easy. He wanted nothing more than to wrap mother and son in his arms, but they weren't his family.

The guys were right, he was too emotionally invested in them. He needed to think and act like a lawman, not as a potential husband and father.

The mistakes he'd made in the past lingered in his mind. Leanne Columbus had come across like an innocent woman in a troubled relationship. Not unlike Mari's situation with her ex-husband. They'd needed key intel on Leanne's boyfriend

Colin Farley related to a murder and she agreed to work with them to set up a meeting because she wanted him arrested. But Leanne had played him for a fool, luring him into a trap that had resulted in her so-called abusive boyfriend shooting at them, nearly killing Tuck and Marsh.

He didn't believe Mari had shot and killed Jeff Abbott. But he really didn't know for sure that she was telling him the truth about her memories of Roy Carlton's activities before his arrest.

Logically, he didn't want to believe she'd purposefully hold back information. Especially knowing her son was in danger.

But he wasn't sure he could trust his judgment either.

He crossed the threshold of the connecting door to put badly needed distance between them. Eyeing the computer, he tried to come up with another way to help investigate the case. They should have known about Cindy Gorlich's financial troubles before now, and he worried that he was dropping the ball on other clues, too. There was so much going on that made it difficult to keep track of everything that needed to be followed up.

He called Tucker. "What's the scoop with the search warrants?"

"Marsh and Jackson are going through Tifton's apartment. They haven't found anything obvious yet, other than it appears the guy hasn't been there lately, as evidenced by old garbage and a small stack of mail."

His gut clenched. "Do you think Tifton is dead?"

"That's one theory. The other is that he skipped town for a few days. When they finish the search, they're going to meet me at Cindy's place. I'm here now, keeping an eye on things until they arrive."

"That's good." There was always the possibility that Cindy might try to destroy evidence. Although if that was her intent, she likely would have done that already. "Is she home?"

"Looks like it," Tuck agreed.

Sam glanced at his watch, wishing he could head out to assist with the search. He almost suggested Marsh and Jackson come to the motel but then remembered how the last time he'd left Mari and Theo, the shooter had tried to take them out.

"Will you keep me updated?"

"Sure thing," Tuck drawled. "How are things at the motel?"

"Quiet." Which was a good thing. Even if it made him feel useless. "Later."

"Later," Tuck agreed.

"Sam?" He turned, sliding his phone into his pocket to find Mari standing in the doorway. "Theo is hungry."

"So am I," he said with a smile. "Let's grab lunch. There's a fast-food restaurant across the street."

"That would be wonderful." Her brow furrowed. "Is it safe for us to leave?"

He hesitated, then shook his head. "Better if I place a carry-out order."

"That works." She smiled wryly. "Theo loves chicken bites. I'll have the grilled chicken sandwich."

"That can be arranged." He used an app on his phone to place their order. Then crossed to the window to scan the parking lot. There was no sign of anyone lurking around. He couldn't see how the gunman could know where they were staying. Even the sheriff's deputies didn't know their location.

And he intended to keep it that way.

Fifteen minutes later, he'd picked up their food and had spread out their meals on the small table in his room, having closed and stored the computer in a shoulder bag.

As always, Mari bowed her head to say grace. He longed to take her hand in his but didn't, following her lead and bowing his head, too. "Dear Lord Jesus, we thank You for the blessings You have bestowed upon us. We humbly ask that You continue to keep us safe in Your care. Amen."

"Amen," Theo said.

"Amen," he echoed. "I like how you focus on the positive side of things," he added. "Especially when it would be easy to wallow in the negative."

"I have faith that God has brought us along this path for a reason." She smiled and unwrapped Theo's chicken bites, breaking them in half, then opened several packets of ketchup. "Be careful, they're hot," she cautioned.

They ate in silence for a moment. He was touched by her faith in God. He remembered how he'd prayed when they were leaving the original ranch house and felt a little ashamed that he'd only done so in a time of extreme need, rather than showing his gratitude for everyday blessings.

"I loved your prayer, Mari. I need to do better."

"Sam, you're doing fine. God is always listening, no matter what." She lightly touched his arm, sending a zing of awareness skipping along his skin. "He knows your heart."

"I hope so." It was all he could do not to lean over and kiss her again. He cleared his throat. "Thanks for reminding me of what is important in life."

"Anytime." Her smile brought another wave of awareness washing over him.

The moment was broken when his phone rang. Sam fished it from his pocket, saw the caller was Tucker, then rose to his feet to move away so as to not disturb Theo. "What's up? Tell me you have something."

"Well, we didn't find anything in Cindy's apartment, but when we confronted her about her financial situation and mentioned that the search warrant included her financial records like her bank statements, she broke down sobbing," Tucker said. "She claimed she was about to be evicted from her apartment when a man contacted her about helping Roy Carlton escape. He offered her ten grand, made in two five grand payments. Desperate to dig herself out of debt, she took him up on the offer."

Sam felt a surge of satisfaction. Finally they were getting somewhere. "Who contacted her? What's his name?"

"She claims he never gave her a name, only referred to himself as one of Roy's friends," Tuck explained. "She said he told her not to ask questions, and she half expected the call to be some sort of scam. But then the first five grand was deposited in her bank account within two hours of the call. That was enough for her. She claimed all she had to do was to leave her keys in the van and declare that it was stolen. She didn't think it was that big of a deal."

"She's wrong. Aiding and abetting an escaped convict is a very big deal," Sam pointed out.

"Oh, I arrested her on the spot, so she is finally seeing the error of her ways," Tuck said with a sigh. "We grilled her hard, but she stuck to her story."

"What about the payments themselves?" he asked.

"Yeah, we have our tech guy tracing the source of the deposit. Seems like it came through some crypto currency account in an offshore bank, so it's going to take some time."

That didn't sound reassuring. Sam had a bad feeling tracing the money would take too long. Every minute the gunman was out there, Mari and Theo remained in danger. He wanted this guy caught and arrested ASAP. "What about the phone number the guy used to contact Cindy? Can we track that?"

"Call came from a disposable cell phone purchased at a discount store with broken security cameras," Tucker said. "From what our tech guy is saying, the phone was used for only a few days in several public areas in the city, before it went dark, likely destroyed. Not helpful as far as narrowing a specific location of our perp."

In other words, another dead end. He blew out a breath, staring out the window at the small parking lot. Who was this anonymous guy claiming to be Roy's friend? Jeff Abbott? It would make sense to have Abbott get Roy out of jail, then to kill him so he couldn't talk.

Carlton must have died for the same reason. To keep him from talking. But why? What did they know? Who was the mastermind behind all of this?

And how did Mari and Theo fit into the puzzle?

"Sam? You still there?" Tucker asked.

"Yeah. But why does it feel like we're no closer to uncovering the truth?" He didn't bother to hide his frustration.

"I hear you," Tucker agreed.

"Do we know for sure Cindy wasn't involved in the shooting incidents?" It occurred to him that ten grand was a lot of money to simply allow a car to be stolen.

"She was out at a local pub the night of the first shooting," Tuck said. "And she was working the following day. We didn't find any weapons, not that she couldn't have gotten rid of it. Still, she's a blubbery mess right now. Honestly, I don't think she is capable of shooting anyone."

"And what about our other search warrant?" Sam pressed. So far, they had nothing to show for the day's work. And very few additional avenues to investigate.

"Unfortunately, Zach Tifton is still missing. Owens has instructed us to reach out to his friends and family to find him."

Again, Sam wished he could be out there,

doing the legwork to follow up on leads. "Okay, but now that we know Cindy Gorlich was paid to let Roy steal her car, Tifton is likely off the hook."

"Possibly, but based on his calling in sick and being missing, boss wants us to tie up that loose end. Hey, speaking of which, Owens is on the other line now. Talk later." With that, Tucker ended the call.

Sam lowered the phone, still staring outside. This case was confounding on so many levels.

Movement from across the parking lot caught his attention. He narrowed his gaze. Was that a man in a ski mask? No rifle this time, but his instincts were screaming at him that this guy was likely armed.

"Mari, grab Theo and go into your room. Hide in the bath, understand? Keep your head down until I come and get you." He'd barely said the words when the crack of gunfire had him jumping back from the window in the nick of time.

A bullet punctured the glass, whizzed past the two double beds to lodge in the wall between the bedroom and bathroom. He drew his weapon, took aim and fired back.

Theo began to cry, gut-wrenching sobs that were difficult to ignore. Sam stood to the side of the window, eyeing the opposite side of the parking lot warily. Returning fire had caused the gunman to drop out of sight.

He was about to tell Mari to call 911, but her voice calm and strong from the other room indicated she already had.

Help would be there soon. He just needed to survive long enough for the local cops to arrive.

THIRTEEN

Stretched out in the bathtub with Theo tucked in front of her, Mari prayed. Theo's crying ripped at her heart, but as much as she tried to reassure him that they were fine, gunfire still echoed around them.

Sam was firing back at the gunman, which gave her hope for their ability to escape yet also made her worry for his safety. She trusted Sam to protect them, and she couldn't bear the thought of losing him.

Please, Lord Jesus! Protect us all!

Hearing the shrill wail of sirens helped her to remain calm. This motel was located just outside of Austin, which meant the police department would respond, rather than the sheriff's deputies.

She still didn't trust the deputies after the incident at the ranch. Roy's dead body had been placed in her living room while the deputy was supposedly outside watching the house.

The sirens were much louder now, and the gunfire had stopped. "The police are here, Theo," she said, pressing a kiss to his head. "We're safe now. The police will keep us safe."

"I want Mr. Sam," Theo sobbed. "And Charlie."

"Charlie is right here." Theo had the dog when she'd picked him up from the bed. She tucked Charlie in closer, frowning a bit when she felt the beginning of a small opening in the stuffed animal's belly. She made a mental note to repair the dog when they got home.

"Mari? Are you and Theo okay?" Sam asked.

"Yes." Her voice sounded hoarse, as if she'd been screaming. She cleared her throat and lifted her head to look over the edge of the tub. "We're not hurt."

Sam stood in the doorway, his gaze full of regret and maybe a hint of anger. Not at her, she knew, but at the situation.

"I need you to stay there for a moment, until the Austin PD clears the area." He hesitated, then added, "I'll be back as soon as possible."

"I understand." Being in the tub wasn't exactly comfortable, but she wasn't about to complain. She knew there could have been more than one shooter outside. And there was evidence to preserve, too.

"I wanna get out of here," Theo whined.

"I know, but we have to wait for Mr. Sam to

come back." She kissed him again. "I know, why don't we sing songs?"

Theo sniffled loudly, then nodded. "Okay. I wanna sing the bus song."

No surprise as it was his favorite. They sang together, for several minutes. When they finished the "Wheels on the Bus" song, she suggested another a church song they'd recently learned, called "Jesus Loves Me."

After three songs, Sam returned. "Sounds like you're ready for the church choir," he said with a smile. He offered her a hand. She took it, grateful for his strength.

Once she'd gotten out of the bathtub, Sam leaned over to lift Theo into his arms. Her son rested his head on Sam's chest. "Was that the scary man?"

"Yes, but he's gone now," Sam said reassuringly. "You don't have to worry about him."

"Why does he keep coming to scare us?" Theo asked, his tear-streaked face tearing her apart.

Sam sent her a panicked gaze, clearly not sure how to answer. Unfortunately, she didn't have a good response to her son's good question either. "We don't know, sweetie, but he'll go to jail for a long time." She didn't add, when they finally caught him.

Thankfully, it was enough to satisfy Theo. He lowered his head back to Sam's chest, content in his arms.

Theo needed a father. She had to tear her gaze away from the image Sam and Theo made, before she broke down sobbing, too.

Charlie was in the bottom of the bathtub, so she bent to scoop him up. Turning the dog over, she poked the bit of stuffing back into the small opening.

Then frowned when she felt something hard and unyielding. What in the world?

Examining the underbelly more closely, she gasped when she felt something move. What was in there? She used his fingers to rip the opening to the point she could pull whatever was in there, out.

A small USB drive plopped into her hand.

"Sam?" She turned to stare at him. "I found this inside Charlie. And I didn't put it there."

Sam's eyebrows levered upward. "Who gave Theo the stuffed animal?"

"Roy." She turned the USB drive over in her hand as if there would be something on the outside that would help explain what it was and why it was in the dog. "He bought the dog when I first discovered I was pregnant. I took it with us when we left, mostly because I wanted Theo to have something from his father."

"May I?" Sam asked holding out his hand.

She dropped the drive in his palm, then pushed the stuffing back inside Charlie. In that moment, she realized this was the reason Roy had tried to kidnap Theo. It wasn't because he'd wanted his son; he was after the USB drive he'd hidden in the dog.

"This is great news, Mari," Sam said, breaking into her thoughts. "Whatever is on this drive is likely the key to blowing this investigation wide-open."

"I hope so." She wished she'd noticed the sutures in Charlie sooner, but who paid attention to a stuffed animal? It had never occurred to her that Roy would do something as crazy as hiding evidence in Theo's toy.

Was this the reason they'd been in nonstop danger?

"We need to get out of here," Sam said in a low voice, interrupting her thoughts. "It's a crime scene, and the techs need to get inside to find the slugs from the weapon."

She wanted to ask about the shooter. "Is he— gone?"

"Yeah. DOA," he admitted. She assumed that meant dead on arrival of the police officers. "We can't interrogate him, but knowing who he is may help us track down who hired him."

"That's good." Not that a man lost his life but having something to go on. For the past few days it has felt as if they were stumbling around in the dark without flashlights.

Maybe now, with the USB drive and the dead gunman, they'd find exactly what they'd need to put an end to this nightmare, once and for all.

One glance at the bullet-ridden wall was sobering. Swallowing hard, she followed Sam and Theo outside to where a slew of police officers were tapping off the crime scene and marking evidence.

Through the throng, she saw Tucker running toward them, concern etched on his features. "Everyone okay?"

"Yeah," Sam said. She noticed he hadn't mentioned the USB drive to the local cops. "We need another place to stay. One that accepts cash with no questions asked."

"I'll have Marsh look into that," Tucker agreed. He raked his gaze over her and then looked with sympathy at Theo. "Rough day."

"You could say that." She tried to keep her tone light, but tears pricked her eyes. Blinking them back, she drew in a deep breath and added, "But God was watching over us and that's all that matters."

"I couldn't agree more," Sam murmured. "Tuck, can you drive us out of here? Hold on, we'll grab Theo's car seat."

"Yes, this way." Once Sam had removed the brand-new seat they'd purchased only a few hours ago, Tucker drew them through the sea of cops to the spot where he'd left his SUV.

To her surprise no one stopped them. "Don't we need to give statements?"

"I told the local cops that we would do that later," Sam said, an edge to his tone. "They didn't like it, but nothing is more important than your safety."

She nodded, grateful for the reprieve. It wasn't as if she had much to tell them anyway. Sam had seen the shooter, then told her to take Theo into the bathtub. And that was all she knew.

Well, except for finding the USB drive.

Sam didn't bring it up until they were all settled in Tucker's SUV and were heading away from the motel crime scene. "As soon as we get settled in another motel, I need you to get a computer."

"What's the rush?" Tucker asked.

"Mari found this." Sam held up the USB drive. "Roy Carlton hid it inside Theo's stuffed dog."

Tucker let out a low whistle. "That's great news. And explains a lot. It could be that the USB drive is the driving force behind these attacks. And why the bedrooms were searched."

"Yeah." Sam tucked the drive back into his pocket. Then he pulled out his phone. "I'll have Jackson get the computer and meet us at the motel."

"Good plan," Tucker agreed. He tapped a message that had come up on the SUV's screen. "Looks like Marsh has secured a place for us. Let Jackson know, okay?"

Mari sat beside Theo, grateful to have the rangers gathered around them. She tried to let go of her anger toward Roy for putting her and their son in danger. There was no point in wishing things were different.

All that mattered was uncovering whatever information was on the USB drive and who was ultimately responsible for shooting at them.

And while she would miss Sam terribly once this was over, she would be more than happy for her life to go back to normal.

Hopefully in time to celebrate the new year and Theo's fifth birthday.

Sam couldn't wait to see what was on the USB drive. He turned to glance at Mari and Theo in the back, grateful to note the little boy seemed calmer now. The way Theo had clung to him after the shooting had been touching. Sam had been reluctant to let him go.

There was no denying the child looked up to him as a father figure. The realization should have scared him, but it didn't.

Just the opposite.

He'd prayed like he'd never prayed before the

entire time Mari and Theo were hiding in the bathtub. God had been watching over him. It was the only explanation as to how he'd hit the shooter, since he'd never gotten a good look at the guy.

The gunman's face hadn't been the least bit familiar, but the first officers on scene noticed the tattoo of a cobra on his arm, which indicated he may be part of a newer drug cartel known as the Rey Cobras, operating near the border. A fact that only muddied the waters of the investigation.

Why on earth was a drug cartel involved? Had Carlton been working for them? And if so, was that the reason Roy Carlton had shot and killed the city manager, Hank George?

"Mr. Sam?" Theo's voice broke into his thoughts.

He turned in his seat. "What do you need?"

"Did you forget my new toys?" Theo's lower lip trembled as if he were about to cry again.

He hid a wince because he had indeed forgotten Theo's new toys. "I—uh, yes, I'm sorry. We'll get you some new ones, okay?"

"More action figures?" Theo asked.

"Absolutely." He wasn't sure when they'd have time to make another run to the store, but he couldn't bring himself to disappoint the little boy. "The same ones we bought before."

"Soon?" Theo asked hopefully.

"Ah—" He glanced helplessly at Mari.

"The new motel room will have the same children's TV station as before," Mari said. "We'll find something fun to watch until it's time to get more toys."

Theo seemed to consider this, then nodded. "Okay."

Crisis averted, Sam thought. He felt terrible for what Theo and Mari were going through. How had the member of a drug cartel found them in the first place? He didn't like any of this and made another promise not to use plastic anywhere near their new location.

He would have preferred a formal safe house, but that would mean going up the chain of command. And he wasn't ready to do that. Oh, he trusted Captain Owens, but the governor's office had been the one to ask for the rangers' help in the first place. And considering this all started with the city manager being murdered, politicians—even the mayor—could be involved.

Yeah, somehow, there seemed to be far too many fingers in this pie. Too bad he wasn't in the mood to share. Not after this latest attack.

"Do you want me to swing past a store?" Tuck asked in a low voice. He waved to the left. "There's a department store up ahead."

Sam hesitated, then shook his head. "Better to wait until later. We need to know what is on this

USB drive." He didn't add his hopes that discovering what was on there might be enough for an arrest and the end to the danger.

He knew Mari would prefer to return to the ranch house as soon as possible.

"Your call," Tuck said with a nod and kept going. Up ahead, Sam could see the name of the motel Marsh had secured for them using cash.

Now if Jackson could just get there with the laptop computer, they'd be all set.

As promised, Marsh was standing outside waiting for them. He held up two room keys and gestured to the door beside him.

Tuck pulled right up to the door and threw the gearshift into Park. Sam pushed out from the passenger seat, then opened the rear doors for Mari and Theo.

"I can do it," Theo said, pushing his hands away. In a spurt of independence, Theo worked on the strap holding him in place.

Mari shrugged, getting out and coming around to stand beside him. Theo released the buckle then scrambled down from the car seat.

"See? I did it all by myself."

"That you did," Mari agreed. "Come inside now, okay?"

Marsh held the first motel room door open for them. The hour was almost three in the afternoon, although it seemed later since they'd been on the move since early that morning. Marsh handed Sam the key. "Connecting rooms," he said. "As requested."

"Thanks. I'll open this side." He followed Mari and Theo into the room, quickly unlocking the connecting door.

"I wanna watch cartoons," Theo said, bouncing on the bed.

"Let's see what they have." Mari pointed the remote at the television. It didn't take long for her to find the children's channel. "Oh, look! This is one of your favorites."

Theo settled down on the bed, clutching Charlie close. Sam hoped the boy would be preoccupied for a while.

"What happened at the motel?" Marsh asked.

Sam quickly filled him in. "I hope Jackson gets here soon with the computer."

"He's five minutes out," Tuck said. "And we should get an ID on the shooter soon, too."

"Too bad we can't question him," Marsh said. "Almost seems as if that entire fiasco was a suicide mission."

"Maybe." Sam frowned. "I hadn't thought of that. You made sure we weren't followed, right?"

"Right." Marsh nodded. "But we need to stay on high alert, regardless. I can't put anything past these guys."

"Yeah. Obviously there is more than one perp

involved." The USB drive was burning a hole in his hand. He stepped up to the window, glad to see Jackson pulling into the motel parking lot. "Jackson's here now."

"I'm nervous," Mari said softly. "I can't imagine what is on that drive."

"Hopefully a full confession," Sam said. Although that didn't make sense. Carlton had already been sent to prison for murdering the city manager. Why bother to break out of jail to hide his own confession?

"Sounds like y'all had a busy day," Jackson drawled as Marsh opened the door to let him in. "What's this about a secret drive?"

"Set the computer down and we'll find out." Sam stepped forward. The moment the computer was turned on, he inserted the USB drive and double-clicked to open it.

Mari, Tuck, Marsh and Jackson all crowded around him. To his surprise, there were several documents on the drive. He opened them in chronological order according to the date, starting with the oldest document first.

"Is he really talking about the Rey Cobras cartel?" Jackson asked.

Sam nodded slowly, feeling a little sick to his stomach as he read what was almost like a journal of Roy's descent into the life of crime. "Roy was recruited by the Rey Cobras, also known as

King Cobra cartel, to sell drugs. The shooter at the motel scene had a cobra tattoo on his arm, which the local cops identified as part of the same cartel." He glanced back at Mari, who had paled at the news. "You didn't know about that?"

"No." Her voice was barely a whisper. "Roy wasn't the greatest husband in the world, but selling drugs? I never would have expected him to do something like that."

Sam knew people desperate for money were easy targets to be drawn into criminal organizations. If Roy's construction company had lost contracts, it would make sense he'd try to do something else to supplement his income.

"How does the King Cobra cartel fit into the murder of Hank George?" Tucker asked.

Sam clicked on the next document, which held more information about the King Cobra cartel, and specifically Roy's contact known as Jose Edwardo. "Marsh, get the name of Jose Edwardo to Owens."

"On it," Marsh agreed.

Sam clicked on the next document. "Okay, this one mentions a person with 'political clout' as being involved. He mentions Jeff Abbott being involved, too, which may explain why he was murdered. There are also meeting dates and times taking place three years ago." He glanced at Tuck and Jackson. "Hank George? His political clout?"

Jackson shrugged. "Then why kill him? I'd lean toward the mayor himself."

"What about the guy who has taken over the city manager's job?" Tucker asked. "What's his name? Doug Granger?"

"Yeah, maybe." Sam wished Roy had been a little more specific. But there were still two more documents to review, so he moved on, clicking on the next document. He frowned at the blank page.

"Do you think he was arrested before he could finish?" Tucker asked.

"I hope not." He minimized that document and clicked on the last and most recent one. Thankfully, it wasn't blank.

And when he began reading, his pulse kicked into high gear. "Roy Carlton claims he was set up to take the fall for Hank George's murder."

"I'm not sure we should believe that," Jackson drawled.

"Normally, I wouldn't, but it's interesting he's writing this but had not used it as part of his defense," Sam said. He kept reading, then sat back. "Check out that last paragraph. He was told he'd be 'richly rewarded' for cooperating and going to jail if convicted." Sam turned in his chair to face Mari. "What do you think?"

She slowly shook her head, looking confused and upset. "I'm shocked Roy would go along with something like that. Giving up two years of his life for money? Roy was not known to be patient."

"They did help him escape," Tucker mused.

"Yeah, then killed him so he couldn't talk." Sam sighed, rubbing his hands over his face. "We need to know which person with political clout is involved."

"And working with a drug cartel," Jackson agreed. "That's a big problem."

Yeah, it was. And Sam had no idea how they'd get the answers they needed.

FOURTEEN

Drugs. Her life and Theo's were in danger because of drugs. Well, that and murder, she silently amended.

The news was shocking, and even now, looking back, she couldn't say that Roy's behavior had ever hinted to the fact he was using drugs.

More likely selling them.

She shivered, hating knowing that Roy had been killed because of sheer greed. Rather than working harder, getting another part-time job, he'd gone down the path of becoming a criminal.

Going as far as doing jail time for the promise of a *rich reward*.

The only encouraging part of reading Roy's notes hidden on his USB drive was that he hadn't murdered anyone. Someday, when Theo was old enough to ask questions about his biological father, she wouldn't have to tell her son his father had killed a man.

Not that selling drugs or getting involved in a drug cartel was much better.

Swallowing hard, she moved away from the small table to check on her son. Engrossed in a children's movie, he didn't seem to notice her hovering in the doorway between their rooms.

Her heart ached for what Theo had been through. Nearly being kidnapped, then shot at multiple times. No wonder he had suffered nightmares.

And likely would for months to come.

"Okay, boss has issued a BOLO for Roy's contact, Edwardo," Marsh said. "He has a criminal record for selling drugs and possession. He was extradited back to Mexico last year, but I assume he snuck back over the border."

She hoped finding Jose Edwardo would help put an end to the danger.

"We need to interview the mayor and this new city manager, Granger," Sam said. "If either of them balks at that, we'll get Owens to pave the way for us."

"Good idea," Tucker agreed. "I'll call the mayor's office now to get the request on record. He's less likely to be available."

Tucker moved past her to make the call. "Hello, Rachel? This is Texas Ranger Tucker Powell. I need a meeting with Mayor Beaumont ASAP." A pause, then he said, "I don't think you understand how important this is. However, I'm sure I can contact my boss Captain Owens to facilitate a meeting, or even the governor's office, if needed." Another pause, then Tucker's expression revealed his satisfaction. "Yes, ma'am, four o'clock this afternoon works just fine. Tell the mayor we will see him, shortly."

Tucker noticed her listening and winked. "Sometimes charm doesn't work and you have to pull out the big guns."

She couldn't help smiling back. "Whatever gets the job done."

"Exactly." His expression sobered. "I'm sorry you and your son are in this position."

"It's okay." Tucker was being sweet, and while she appreciated his kindness, she couldn't help glancing over at Sam. He was the one she cared about, far more than she should. "I know you will protect us."

Tucker nodded and moved back to the group. "We're set for four o'clock this afternoon. We'll need to come up with something more other than the USB drive to convince Beaumont to cooperate with us."

"I was thinking about that," Sam said. "If we believe Carlton's claim that he didn't kill Hank George, then who did? With the DNA evidence and his fingerprints on the murder weapon, the investigation stopped, right?"

"Yeah," Marshall said. "I see where you're going. We know Hank George was killed in his home but left in an alley behind a restaurant. We need to pick up where the cops left off, searching for video from neighbors' homes and/or businesses in the area where his body was found. They probably didn't bother to keep going after getting Carlton in custody."

"Let's do it," Jackson said. "We don't have a lot of time."

"We'll spread out," Tucker agreed. "I'll take the businesses closest to the dump site. Marshall, you and Jackson go back and canvass the homes in Hank George's neighborhood."

"I'm in," Jackson said without hesitation.

Mari could tell Sam wanted to go with them, but of course he nodded. "I'll stay here, but if you find something send it to me and I'll put it with the other information we have." He gestured to the computer. "I'll also send the documents we found on the USB drive to Owens."

"Good. We're getting closer to uncovering the truth, I can feel it." Jackson reached for the door. "We'll keep in touch."

"Later," Sam said, as the three rangers headed out.

There was a long moment of silence when they were alone again. She told herself not to think

about their kiss but to stay focused on the investigation. "What are you going to do now?"

"Dig into social media again." Sam shrugged.
"I've been checking Doug Granger's postings,
but so far I haven't seen anything remotely suspicious. From what I can tell, the guy is clean. We'll
still interview him, but the mayor seems a more
likely candidate with his election coming up."

"What about the mayor's social media?" She
moved closer and dropped into the second chair.
"Maybe we'll learn something there?"

"It's possible." Sam sat beside her. "I doubt
he'll be in pictures with cartel members but it's
worth a shot."

She leaned forward to see the screen as he
began to search. There were dozens of posts for
Mayor Beaumont, including several fundraisers
for his reelection campaign. She tapped one of the
photographs. "Do you think his needing funds
for his campaign is a part of this?"

"Maybe." Sam continued poking around.
"Looks like Beaumont has at least a few deputies supporting him."

She frowned. "That seems odd. Why the sheriff's department? Austin city is protected by the
Austin Police Department. The sheriff's department only has jurisdiction within the courthouse,
at the jail and in the counties that are outside of
Austin. Including Whistling Creek Ranch."

"True," Sam scowled. "We already know the deputies goofed up protecting Carlton in the hospital. And let Carlton's dead body get placed in your house." He turned to meet her gaze. "Goes back to our original thought that maybe one of them or more are dirty."

She nodded, not wanting to believe it, but couldn't ignore the deputy on the screen shaking hands with Mayor Beaumont as if they were good buddies.

Maybe they just golfed together. Or had friends in common. Yet when she leaned forward, she noticed the deputy looked familiar. She put her hand on Sam's arm to stop him from scrolling. "Wait a minute, I think that's Deputy Strawn. You remember, he was the one who responded to my call that first night when Roy tried to kidnap Theo. He seemed nice and concerned about the event."

"Interesting, but not exactly proof of wrongdoing," Sam said. "Let's keep looking for connections."

"Mommy, my movie is over," Theo called.

She reluctantly stood. "I'll see if I can find something else for him to watch."

Sam nodded without looking up from the computer screen. The sense of camaraderie seemed to have evaporated. She told herself it didn't matter as they were working to find those responsible for shooting at them.

Stepping into the next room, she found Theo standing in front of the television, moving from one foot to the other. "Do you have to go to the bathroom?"

He nodded and quickly ran toward it. She sighed and took the remote. She didn't like Theo to have so much screen time, but without other toys to keep him occupied she didn't have much of a choice.

Better screen time than to risk going back to the store.

It didn't take long to find another children's movie. When Theo returned, she lifted him up onto the bed. "Would you like to watch this show?"

He nodded and leaned against her. She held him close for a moment, silently thanking God for keeping him safe.

Yet the nonstop danger was wearing her down. This was their second motel in one day. All she could do was to hope and pray Tucker was right about how they were getting closer to uncovering the truth.

Before anyone else got hurt.

Ignoring Mari and Theo was impossible. The moment Mari left to tend to her son, he'd wanted

224 Texas Kidnapping Target

to follow. As if she needed his help to find a new TV program for her son.

He could've asked one of the other guys to stay behind but had chosen to keep his mouth shut. *Not a smart move, Hayward*, he inwardly railed. He should have taken the opportunity to put distance between them. Instead, he'd stayed put.

He was flailing in the deep end of the pool when it came to Mari and her son. They'd managed to wiggle their way into his heart despite his efforts to remain professional.

Giving himself a mental shake, he scrolled through the photos on Mayor Beaumont's page. Other than Deputy Strawn being acquainted with the guy, nothing else stood out as suspicious.

He switched his attention from the mayor to the newly appointed city manager, Doug Granger. Maybe Hank George had been killed because he learned about something criminal going on within the city. And they needed someone who would look the other way, like Doug Granger, in that position instead.

Yet why? That was the part that didn't make any sense. What power did the city manager have?

Maybe building permits? Hadn't Roy Carlton been working construction? He began to dig into Longhorn Construction, the company Mari had mentioned, but there was very little information on the internet about them.

He pulled out his phone to make sure he hadn't missed a call. Nope, the guys hadn't found anything, or if they had, they hadn't clued him in. And the meeting with Mayor Beaumont was barely ninety minutes from now.

For a long moment he stared at the computer. What were they missing? A member of the King Cobra drug cartel had pummeled their motel room with bullets. Roy was set up to take the fall on killing Hank George.

Maybe Mari was right about Mayor Beaumont needing a source of funding for his campaign. He brought up information on state and local campaign donations. Of course, Texas didn't have any regulations relative to how much money could be given via an anonymous donation.

Was it as simple as the mayor getting campaign funds from sketchy sources? Like directly from the drug cartel, itself? If so, why? He didn't quite understand the motive. The mayor of Austin had some power when it came to running the city, but he was accountable to the city council. It wasn't like the mayor could turn his back on a sudden influx of illegal drugs. But maybe there were some ways Beaumont could allow members of the drug cartel to operate in the city.

Wait a minute. He straightened in his seat, going back to the website of Longhorn Construction. Was it possible the company was involved?

According to Roy, they'd lost a key contract for a new project.

In searching new construction sites, he identified a company by the name of Tribeca Construction. They had a more robust website, with several photos of other projects they'd completed. Tribeca looked legit, whereas Longhorn seemed a bit sketchy.

He went back to the City of Austin website and found the meeting minutes for their council meetings. As he scanned them, he felt Mari come up behind him.

"What are you looking at?" she asked, leaning over his shoulder.

"Council meeting minutes, going back to about the time the city manager was killed." She was close enough that if he turned his head, he could kiss her. "I'm wondering if this isn't related to contracts with construction companies. Like Longhorn, the one Roy worked for, and this one, Tribeca Construction."

Mari didn't say anything but stayed behind him, reading over his shoulder. He worked hard not to let her distract him.

"Here, this meeting was three months before the murder," he said. "And look at that, City Manager Hank George has expressed concerns over Longhorn Construction for what he deemed were worrisome business practices. He insisted they use Tribeca Construction instead."

"And then he was murdered, allegedly by Roy," Mari said. "I remember something about how Roy was accused of acting out of a fit of anger and revenge in killing Hank. Because he and several of his fellow workers had lost their jobs."

"Yeah. Only now we know Roy didn't kill him, and that this could all be related to the King Cobra drug cartel." There were still some puzzle pieces missing. Then it came to him. "Maybe the cartel owns Longhorn Construction."

Mari finally moved away to sit in the chair beside him. She frowned. "Why would they bother with a legitimate business? Unless it's about laundering drug money."

"That is possible, but I was thinking more about bringing materials in and out of Mexico which would enable them to move drugs at the same time." He reached for his phone. "And people like employees coming in and out might not be searched for drugs either. I need to update Owens. I think there's more than enough here to get the governor's attention."

He quickly gave Captain Owens the bit of information he'd learned about the construction angle. "Good work, Hayward. Keep digging."

"That's the plan," he agreed. "Have you heard from Tuck, Marsh or Jackson?"

"Not yet," Owens admitted. "Could be there isn't any helpful video footage."

That was possible, although these days many people had ring doorbell cameras. "Okay, I'll be in touch if I find out anything more."

"Oh, one more thing," Owens said. "We have an ID on the shooter you took out at the motel. It's the same guy you told me to issue a BOLO for, Jose Edwardo."

He inwardly groaned. "So that name is nothing more than another dead end."

"Afraid so. Although the local cops did confirm his ties to the King Cobra cartel."

"That's no surprise, considering the cobra tattoo. Thanks."

Owens grunted in response and ended the call. As he set the phone down, Mari looked at him. "Jose Edwardo was Roy's contact, right? I guess it's no surprise he was the shooter."

"Yeah, it's one more connection." And he really wished the guy was still alive to interrogate. Then he thought about the medical examiner working on Roy Carlton's body. He made another call and was put straight through.

"Dr. Bond? Ranger Sam Hayward. Do you know if gunpowder residue was found on Carlton's hands or clothes?"

"Not on the hands," Earl Bond confirmed. "The techs took the clothes."

"Thanks." He lowered the phone. "Sounds like Roy might not have been the shooter, although I believe he was the one who tried to kidnap Theo. He knew he'd hidden the USB drive in the dog, no one else did."

"I think so, too." Mari frowned. "What about the meeting with the mayor? Are you going to tell Tucker and the others to ask specifically about Longhorn Construction?"

"They can ask but I'm sure the mayor will deny having anything to do with them." He shrugged. "According to the meeting minutes, it was Hank's decision to stop using them, not his."

"But that's the point, isn't it?" Mari asked with a frown. "If the mayor is using dirty drug money to fund his campaign, he would want Longhorn Construction to get the contracts."

She was right. He reached for his phone and called Tucker. The call went to voice mail. He left a message, then tried Marsh, next. He didn't answer either.

Fighting panic, he reached out to Jackson. Thankfully, he answered. "Something wrong?"

"I tried Tuck and Marsh but they didn't answer. Are you doing okay out there?"

"Are you checking up on us?" Jackson sounded testy. "As far as I know, everything is fine. They're probably busy, hopefully reviewing video. What do you need?"

"I just wanted you to be aware of another angle to this whole mess, prior to your meeting with the mayor." He quickly filled Jackson in on the construction company information. "This is all stuff that should have come out during the initial investigation into Hank Gorge's murder but didn't."

"We can follow up with Beaumont," Jackson agreed. "But don't expect him to suddenly confess."

"I won't. Although you may want to mention how dangerous it would be to get involved with the King Cobra cartel, or any cartel for that matter," Sam said. "He's asking for trouble."

"Will do. Look, I need to go. I have two more houses to check before we meet with the mayor."

"Take care of yourself." Sam disconnected the call and stared at the computer screen for a long moment.

Yeah, the more he considered the implication of the cartel being involved, the more he didn't like it. Cartel members were known to be brutal and vicious. The last thing he wanted was for any of them to continue coming after Mari and Theo.

As much as he hated knowing he'd killed a man, he was glad there was one less shooter to threaten Mari.

Yet there could be others. He abruptly stood and went to the window, scanning the parking lot. Mari's fingers tapped on the keyboard, but he stayed where he was. Maybe he should have asked one of the guys to stay behind, with them.

His phone rang, and he was relieved to see Tucker's name on the screen. "Hey, did you find something?"

"I did. I have a ring doorbell camera from two doors down from Hank George's house. Apparently the owners were gone during the time of the murder, so they were never interviewed by the cops."

"Don't keep me in suspense," Sam said dryly. "What does it show?"

"The video shows a young Hispanic man guy walking down the street toward Hank's house late at night. There's one streetlight that gives a brief glimpse of his profile, but the rest of the angle isn't great. There's no video of him pulling the trigger, but he does walk straight up to the house within thirty minutes of the estimated time of death." Tucker paused, then added, "He looks similar to the shooter from the motel. I'm sending it to the lab to see if they can sharpen the image to say for sure."

"Jose Edwardo," Sam said thoughtfully. "He was Roy's contact within the cartel. And now he's dead."

"Yeah, I know. Mighty convenient if you ask me," Tucker drawled.

"I'm getting the feeling the person with political clout is getting rid of the evidence, including anyone who might be tempted to talk to the authorities." Sam didn't like it one bit. "You better get to that meeting. Maybe you can scare Beaumont into talking if he's the one involved."

"We'll do our best," Tucker promised. "By the way, we're sending Marsh back to your motel. We don't need three of us to do this interview. And we don't like leaving you there alone."

"Okay, we'll watch for Marsh." He wasn't about to complain. "Call me when the interview is finished."

"Will do." Tuck ended the call.

He lowered his phone, then glanced over to where Mari was staring at the computer screen. The intensity of her gaze drew him closer. "Did you find something?"

"I found another picture of Mayor Beaumont with Deputy Strawn," she said. "There's a woman standing between them. She isn't tagged in the photo, so I'm not sure who she is."

"Let me see that." It was his turn to lean over Mari's shoulder. The date and time of the photograph was from November of last year. More than a year ago.

The woman looked familiar, but he couldn't place her. She wasn't Cindy Gorlich, but maybe another hospital employee? Although that didn't make sense, since Deputy Strawn wasn't the one who had been standing guard over Roy during his escape. That had been Deputy Erickson.

He straightened, his mind racing. He had seen this woman before, but when? And where?

Was it possible she was the key to blowing this case wide-open?

FIFTEEN

"Mommy, I'm hungry!"

"Coming." She glanced at her watch, realizing it was past Theo's usual dinner time. "Is there a vending machine or someplace we can get pretzels or crackers for him?"

"Yeah, I'll find something." Sam stood and reached for the door. Then glanced at her over his shoulder. "Don't open the door for anyone, not even the maid. Marsh should be here, soon."

"I won't." She crossed the threshold to join Theo. "Mr. Sam is going to find a snack. Is your show over?"

"No, but I'm hungry." He held up the dog. "Charlie is hungry, too."

She smiled. "I'm glad you have Charlie to keep you company."

That was the wrong thing to say, because it reminded Theo of the toys they'd left behind. She swallowed a sigh when he asked for his action figures again, and his horses.

She wanted to tell him to be content with being safe but didn't. "I know, sweetie. We'll get to the store soon."

Theo huffed and threw himself backward on the bed. "Soon is never," he pouted.

He wasn't entirely wrong about that. She had no idea if it would be safe enough to stop by a store to get a few things. She had the impression Sam was waiting to see how the meeting went with the mayor before making those decisions.

"I'm sorry, but we're waiting for Mr. Marsh to return." It was the best she could do.

Hearing the door opening from the other room, she crossed over to check on Sam. He held up a mini bag of pretzels. "Will this work?"

"Perfect, thanks." She opened the bag and carried them to Theo. "Look, Mr. Sam found pretzels."

"Yum." Theo eagerly took one and popped it into his mouth. He'd get crumbs on the bed but that was the least of her worries.

"Be good for a little while longer, okay?" She gestured to the television. "Watch your movie."

Theo nodded, the pretzels doing the trick. She hurried over to the next room.

Sam was back at the computer, scrolling through the sheriff's department website. She sat beside him. "Who are you looking for?"

"The woman in the photo." Sam glanced at her.

"She looks familiar, but I can't place her. I found Deputy Strawn here on the list of deputies—his first name is Joe." He clicked off that page and went back to social media. "It's a stretch, but he might have a social media presence. Most cops don't, but some do."

"Safety reasons?" she guessed.

He nodded. "No point in making it easy for someone to find you."

She could understand that. She watched as he found several Joe Strawns, but none that lived in the area.

"Nothing," he said with a sigh.

"She's not the mayor's wife?"

"No." He went back to Mayor Beaumont's publicity page. "This is Arianna."

The slender blonde woman standing beside her husband didn't look anything like the short and stocky, dark-haired woman standing between Deputy Strawn and the mayor. "She looks much younger than Beaumont," she observed.

"Yeah, second wife." Sam frowned. "I don't remember there being any sort of scandal about his divorce from the first wife."

She sat back in her seat. "Why would he get himself mixed up with the cartel?"

"We don't know for sure he is, but money is the most common motivator."

"I guess." She couldn't imagine crossing that

line for what had to be a stressful job in the first place. Give her the quiet ranch life any day.

A knock at the door startled her. Sam jumped up, used the peephole, then opened the door. "Hey, Marsh."

"Mommy! My show is over!" Theo called.

She grimaced. "I'm afraid he's tired of watching movies and cartoons."

"We can head out to pick up a few things," Marshall offered. "We'll need to grab food for dinner, anyway. Should be safe enough while the guys are meeting with the mayor."

"Really?" She turned toward Sam, who nodded. "That would be wonderful. I'm sorry it's been so difficult with Theo. He's used to having his own toys and attending his preschool classes. If we were home, I'd set up a play date for him."

"You don't have to apologize, Mari," Sam murmured. "I wish we could put an end to the danger once and for all."

She did, too. "Thanks. I'll get Theo's coat."

As she dressed Theo in his winter gear, she heard Sam and Marsh discussing the case in a low rumble of voices. She couldn't help but wonder if the mayor was really involved or someone else.

Roy had mentioned someone with political clout. He could have at least written down initials.

She suppressed a sigh as she shrugged into her coat. Maybe Tucker and Jackson would get something from their meeting with the mayor.

"Enhanced video confirms it," Marsh was saying as she and Theo went into their room. "Jose Edwardo is the one who approached Hank George's home the night of the shooting."

"Too bad the cops didn't investigate further," Sam muttered. "That would have been enough for reasonable doubt."

"Not necessarily, with having DNA and the murder weapon with Roy Carlton's prints." Marshall shook his head. "I can't say that I blame them. And even if they had seen this guy on the doorbell camera, doesn't mean they would have suspected him of being the shooter."

"I guess you're right," Sam agreed. He met her gaze, then smiled at Theo. "Are you ready to get some toys?"

"Yeah! Toys!" Theo jumped up and down with excitement. Then he cocked his head to the side. "Are these my birthday presents?"

"Yes, these are birthday presents from me and Mr. Marsh," Sam said, ignoring her frown. "But you need to be a good boy, okay? And that means listening to your mom."

"I will!" Theo continued hopping from one foot to the next. "Billy the elf knows I'm a good boy."

"Settle down," she said. "Or we won't go."

Marsh went out of the room first, glancing around before moving away from the doorway. She went next, with Theo beside her with Sam covering them. A few minutes later, they were settled in Marsh's SUV and heading to the store they'd passed on the way to the motel.

The trip to the store didn't take long. Of course, Theo wanted several toys and action figures.

"Pick two," she said firmly. "One present from Mr. Marsh and one from Mr. Sam."

Sam looked as if he might argue, but she narrowed her gaze in warning. Theo couldn't have everything he wanted. Besides, he had two presents waiting for him at home.

Although she really did wish they'd be able to return to the ranch sooner than later.

They were on their way to a fast-food restaurant when Sam's phone dinged. He pulled out his phone and grimaced.

"Bad news?" she asked.

"Yeah. According to Tuck, the meeting with the mayor was short and not very sweet. The guy insisted he knows nothing and became annoyed when they pointed out how a member of the drug cartel was shot and killed outside your motel, Mari. And he also said he has nothing to do with which construction companies get building contracts. They were in and out within fifteen minutes. And that was after he'd made them wait almost an hour to meet with him."

"That's a bummer," Marsh said. "I guess it was too much to hope he'd give anything away."

"Yeah. Traffic is a snarled mess, so the guys are stopping at headquarters to update Owens before heading out to meet us at the motel." Sam turned in his seat to look at her. "I'm sorry we don't have better news."

"It's not your fault." She had hoped for more, but it wasn't like they weren't trying. "Nothing else from other cameras in the area?"

"Oh, yeah, there was a text here about a black truck being seen near the restaurant ten minutes before Hank George's body was found." He shrugged. "Could be the same one I saw being used by the shooter, but they didn't get a plate number either, so there's no way to trace it."

Another dead end. She tried not to show the depths of her despair. They'd already found and examined the information on the USB drive Roy had hidden inside Charlie. What else did these men want with her and her son?

"Maybe they should have told the mayor about the USB drive," she said. "There's no reason for them to keep coming after us."

The two men exchanged a look. "I don't know if that's good enough," Marshall said. "But we'll discuss the idea with our boss."

"Roy knew he hid the USB drive in the dog," Sam said thoughtfully. "But the mayor and whoever else is involved might believe he told you something incriminating."

"I don't know anything!" Her voice came out sharper than she intended. "I wish I could tell them that face-to-face."

Marshall pulled up to the drive-through window. "Let's order and discuss our options when we get back to the motel."

"Sure." She couldn't help feeling dejected. It seemed for all their efforts they were right back where they'd started.

Sam could tell Mari was at the end of her rope. The stress of being in danger, along with the lack of progress on the investigation, was taking a toll.

He wanted nothing more than to wrap her into his arms and reassure her that everything would work out. But it wasn't smart to make promises he might not be able to keep either. All they could do was to keep praying for safety and guidance.

"Grab extra food for Tucker and Jackson, too," he suggested.

"Will do." Soon the enticing scent of burgers and fries filled the interior of the SUV, making his mouth water. Marsh made the short trip back to the motel in record time.

"I'm hungry," Theo said, scrambling from the vehicle.

"Don't forget your action figures," Mari said dryly. "You wanted them, remember?"

"Oh, yeah." Theo came back for them. "My heroes are hungry," he declared.

He and Marsh hung back so Mari and Theo could sit at the table. He bowed his head, waiting for Mari to say grace.

"Dear Lord Jesus, we ask You to please keep us all safe in Your care. Please guide us to the truth. Amen."

"Amen," he echoed, knowing they desperately needed the truth to be revealed. How else could they eliminate the threat to Mari and Theo?

"What do you think about getting the USB drive information out there," Marsh asked in a low voice. They were sitting on the edge of the bed eating their burgers. "She might be right about the danger being over once the bad guys know we found the USB drive hidden by Carlton."

"I would feel better if Roy's USB drive actually named the person with political clout," he said. "I mean, as it stands now, there isn't much to go on."

"No, but the reverse is true, too, isn't it?" Marsh asked. "I mean, what information could Mari have that wouldn't have already been revealed?"

He made a good point. "We might need to talk to Roy's cell mate. Maybe Roy said something to him about who was involved."

"That's possible." Marsh sighed. "But prison snitches aren't exactly good witnesses. The general public is far more likely to believe the mayor's version of the story, rather than someone who'd been convicted of a crime."

"That's true. Unless of course we can find other evidence to support his claim." Sam abruptly straightened. "Maybe we need to head back to the ranch house. Someone searched the place—maybe Roy did hide something in Theo's room."

He hadn't realized Mari was listening in until she turned in her seat to glare at them. "I told you, Roy didn't live with us in the ranch house. I went there to live with my father after leaving him. I filed for separation, got an order of protection before filing for divorce."

She had said that, but he couldn't let the idea go. "Are you saying Roy was never in the ranch house for a family gathering? A holiday? Never?"

"Yes, he was there briefly," she admitted. "But I don't see why he would hide something there."

For the same reason Roy hid the USB drive in Charlie, he thought, but didn't say. "When was the last time he was at the ranch?"

She took a moment to think about that. "Three years ago at Christmas," she admitted. "We were already split up but he showed up unannounced to give Theo a gift. A toy truck," she hastened to add, "So nothing that could have something inside. And he was only in the house for five minutes, and never alone. My dad made it clear he wasn't welcome. There wasn't time for him to have gone into Theo's room to hide anything."

Was he on the wrong track here? Maybe.

"He was arrested just two weeks later," she added. "And from that point forward we had no contact until the divorce was final and I was granted sole custody of Theo." She scowled. "I don't think there's anything at the house."

Before he could respond, his phone rang. "Tuck," he said, glancing at the screen. "What's up?"

"We found Zach Tifton," Tucker announced. "Unfortunately, he's dead. Murdered in almost the exact same way Carlton was, bullet hole in the center of his forehead."

"How?" he demanded. "We never found anything that connected him to Carlton's escape."

"I don't know, but we're heading to the crime scene now," Tucker said. "Just wanted you to know we won't be there anytime soon."

"That's fine. Marsh is here and there's been no sign of anyone lurking around." He couldn't believe Tifton was dead. Murdered. "Keep us informed, will you?"

Laura Scott 245

"Yep. Later." Tuck disconnected the call.

"What happened?" Mari asked.

"Another murder." He glanced at Theo, but thankfully the little boy was eating and playing with his action figure at the same time. "Zach Tifton, another employee at the hospital."

She paled then shook her head. "That doesn't make any sense."

She had that right. He finished his meal, then balled up the garbage. Sitting around in the motel room wasn't going to get them the answers they needed.

He really wanted to head back to Mari's ranch house. Or at least, send Marsh.

As if reading his mind, Marsh nodded. "I can head over there alone but it might be better for us to stick together."

He hesitated, trying to decide what was better for Mari and Theo. "Together," he finally said. "I think that's for the best."

"Okay." Marsh didn't argue. "Let's do it."

Mari's expression was troubled as she cleaned up the mess from their dinner. She went into the bathroom for a wet washcloth and wiped Theo's face and hands.

He caught her hand, offering a reassuring smile. "We'll be fine. No one knows where we are or have reason to believe we're heading back to the ranch."

"I trust you," she said in a low voice. "I just think it's a waste of time."

Maybe it was, but so was sitting around the motel for the rest of the evening. Tuck and Jackson might get something from the crime scene of Tifton's murder, but if not?

They still had nothing to prove Mayor Beaumont was involved with the cartel, and with these recent murders. Jeff Abbott was his stepson—why had he been killed, too? Just because of his friendship with Roy?

Maybe. It was beginning to look as if the answer to keeping the association with the cartel a secret was to kill anyone who might know something incriminating.

Which brought him right back to the attempts on Mari and Theo. Roy could have said something to them, and therefore the mayor and/or his associates wanted her silenced.

Permanently.

"Having second thoughts?" Marsh asked, as Mari took Theo into the bathroom. "We don't have to go."

"I want this to be over for them." He gestured to the connecting room. "Don't you think it's strange they're still in danger?"

"Yeah, but it doesn't sound like Roy had a chance to hide anything either." Marsh shrugged. "The offer still stands for me to go alone."

"Or we wait until Tuck and Jackson are finished with the Tifton crime scene." Sam sighed. "Be honest. Am I just looking for an excuse to get out of here?"

Marsh held his gaze for a moment. "I think you would do just about anything for those two." He jerked his thumb in the direction of Mari and Theo's room. "And you won't rest until you know for sure there's nothing at the ranch house that might help us get to the bottom of this. I agree we need to double-check to make sure."

He nodded slowly. "We'll do everything possible to keep them safe."

"That we will," Marsh agreed.

"We're ready," Mari said, bringing Theo into their room. They were both dressed in their winter coats and Theo was holding on to one of his action figures.

"Okay, great." He shook off the sliver of apprehension. "Like earlier, Marsh will go out first. Mari, you and Theo will follow him, okay?"

Mari nodded and moved closer to Marsh. He opened the door, glanced around for a moment before moving through. Mari and Theo stayed close behind him.

Sam was the last one out. A tall man stepped out from the shadows and he froze, recognizing Deputy Joe Strawn.

Then Sam quickly moved toward the cop, pulling his weapon in a smooth movement and placing himself in front of Mari and Theo. "Stop where you are, Strawn. Don't make me shoot."

"Why would you shoot a cop?" Strawn asked. The deputy was still half in the shadow, making it difficult to see if he was holding a gun down at his side. "I'm here to talk to you and Ms. Lynch."

"No." He heard the sound of Marsh urging Mari and Theo toward the SUV but didn't dare take his gaze off the deputy. "Throw down your weapon and put your hands in the air."

For a long moment the deputy didn't move. Then he lifted his right arm. There was a gun in his hand, the barrel pointing in his direction.

"Stop!" Sam shouted. But Strawn didn't listen. Strawn moved slightly forward, enough for him to see the guy's resigned gaze. The way he moved with excruciating slowness, it was almost as if he wanted Sam to shoot him,

"Drop the weapon," Sam repeated, his tone desperate. "It doesn't have to end like this."

Strawn simply aimed his weapon at Sam, and sensing his finger tightening on the trigger, Sam had no choice but to fire. The bullet from his weapon slammed into Strawn's chest, sending the deputy stumbling backward against the wall of the building. He slowly slid to the ground.

Only then did Strawn drop his gun.

SIXTEEN

"Joe! No, Joe!" a woman shouted. Recognizing Deputy Joe Strawn as the man Sam shot, Mari turned to see a small, dark-haired woman running toward the fallen deputy an expression of sheer anguish on her face.

What in the world? It appeared as if they were a couple, the way she sobbed over his inert body.

"Get inside," Marsh growled near her ear. Theo was thankfully inside the SUV already, and Marsh stood close behind her but she didn't budge. She didn't understand what had just happened. Why the deputy had stood there, as if waiting for Sam to shoot him?

Suddenly another man stepped forward, lifting his weapon toward Sam. Without thinking, she broke past Marshall's arm and rushed the gunman.

"Get back!" Sam yelled, but it was too late. She hit the stranger hard, barely registering that he wasn't the mayor as they'd originally thought.

Her body collided with his. She landed on top

of him, hard enough to make teeth rattle. The man with the gun tried to shove her aside, lifting the weapon in his hand again.

"Stop! Police!" Marshall ran forward just as the gunman fired in Sam's direction. The gunshot was so loud she couldn't hear anything for a long moment. Sam ducked and rolled again to avoid being hit.

Please, Lord Jesus keep Sam safe!

The desperate prayer echoed in her mind seconds before Marshall ran forward, grabbing the weapon from the gunman's grip. "You idiot!" The gunman screamed in fury, his gaze locked on Strawn. "You could have shot them all! You failed the mission!"

Was he talking to Deputy Strawn? Maybe. It was hard to tell with the dark-haired woman weeping over the injured deputy.

"Shut up, Granger. You're under arrest for the attempted murder of a Texas Ranger, and any other charges I can add down the line. You have the right to remain silent and I strongly suggest you use it," Marshall said.

Granger? It took her a moment to place the name. Doug Granger was the newly appointed city manager.

Did that mean Mayor Beaumont wasn't involved? Or were the two of them working together? She grimaced as Marshall yanked Granger to his feet, continuing to read him his rights.

Shaken by the events, Mari pushed herself up and off the asphalt parking lot to limp toward Sam. But then she stopped, realizing Theo was crying her name in the back of the SUV.

"Mommy! Mommy!"

"I'm here. I'm fine, see?" Turning away from Sam, she hurried over to the SUV, pulling him up from the back seat and gathering him close. "I love you, Theo. I love you. Everything will be okay." She kissed the top of his head as his arms gripped her tightly around the neck.

She rocked him back and forth, whispering soothing words as his cries slowly subsided to hiccupping sobs.

"Are you hurt?" Sam called.

She shook her head, unable to speak. That had been close. Far too close. Sam looked as if he'd come to her side, but then abruptly turned to move toward the fallen deputy.

The short, dark-haired woman was still sobbing, her head down on his shoulder.

From where she stood with Theo, she watched Sam check for a pulse, then drop his chin to his chest in a gesture of defeat. In that moment, she understood the deputy was dead.

After a long moment, Sam stood and crossed back toward her and Theo.

"No vest?" Marshall asked, after he'd cuffed Doug Granger's wrists behind his back.

"No. He wanted me to shoot him," Sam said in a low voice. "I just wish I knew why."

"Maybe he thought death was better than facing the cartel," Marshall said.

"I guess." Sam glared at Granger, but the city manager remained silent.

"Joe did it for me." The dark-haired woman lifted her head, tears streaking her face. Mari recognized her from the photograph in which she'd stood between Strawn and the mayor. "He did it for me and our daughter, Ashley. To protect us."

"You're married?" Sam asked. The sound of police sirens filled the air, no doubt called in by other patrons of the motel.

She nodded, sniffling hard. "Yes. And we were forced to help…" Her voice drifted off. Then she added, "I work for Mayor Beaumont."

"Are you Rachel?" Marshall asked. "His administrative assistant?"

She nodded again, avoiding looking at Mari and Theo, likely out of guilt. Rachel had to know that her husband had come here for the sole purpose of killing them.

Instead, he'd sacrificed himself.

"I'm afraid you're under arrest, too," Marshall said, stepping forward. "I assume your boss is in on all of this?"

Rachel grimaced and looked away without responding. Mari tore her gaze from the grief-stricken woman, knowing she needed to work on forgiveness. Maybe later. Right now, she was too numb to feel even a little sympathy for her.

"No more guns, Mommy," Theo whispered. "No more."

"We're safe now," she murmured, wishing she could reassure the little boy that he'd never see or hear another gun. But she wasn't sure if their nightmare was really over. Sam had killed Deputy Strawn and they'd arrested Doug Granger, but if Mayor Beaumont was still involved, wouldn't they need proof to bring him down?

And if so, how long would that take? Hours? Days? Weeks?

She couldn't bear to think about it.

"Where's your daughter now?" Marshall asked as he placed plastic straps around Rachel's wrists. "Is she safe?"

"She's with my mother." Rachel Strawn stared at the ground for a moment, then finally added, "I'll tell you everything you need to know if you make sure my daughter is safe."

"We can do that," Marshall agreed. "What's your mother's name and where does she live?"

"Marion Cummings and she lives in San Antonio." Rachel gave Marshall the address.

He nodded, pulled his phone from his pocket. "Tuck? I need you and Jackson to get to San Antonio ASAP, to take a Marion Cummings and a young girl named Ashley into protective custody."

"Thank you." More tears welled in Rachel's eyes. "We were only supposed to help with hiding the true origin of the campaign funds, but then Joe was told to eliminate the threat or risk our daughter being taken to Mexico and now..." Her voice trailed off again.

And now Joe Strawn was dead.

"As a deputy, he should have known better. He should have come to us," Sam said. "We could have helped him."

Rachel winced and looked away. "Joe was addicted to painkillers after being shot on the job two years ago. The mayor found out about it and threatened to leak the information so he'd lose his job and his pension if he didn't cooperate."

"Better fired than dead," Sam shot back. "I didn't want to shoot him."

"I know. I was afraid he would do something like this. That's why I followed him here." She sniffed again, her gaze going back to her husband. "I guess he's not in pain any longer."

Sam and Marshall exchanged a grim look. The local police arrived then, preventing further conversation. To get out of the way, Mari took Theo back into the motel room, leaving Sam and Marshall to speak with the authorities.

It sounded as if Rachel would testify against

Mayor Beaumont. Would that be enough to ensure her and Theo's safety?

She prayed it would. Because right now, she wanted nothing more than to go home, putting this horror and grief behind them.

Even if that meant leaving Sam. As much as she liked, no—*loved* and respected him, she couldn't add to Theo's stress level. The little boy would suffer nightmares enough as it was. Especially now that he was afraid of guns.

The best thing for her son would be to return to their normal routine.

One that didn't include Sam Hayward.

Sam couldn't get the image of Joe Strawn's resigned gaze out of his mind. He kept replaying the sequence of events over and over in his head, wondering if he could have done something different.

Each time, he came to the same conclusion. The deputy had chosen his path. It hurt to know that in those last few seconds Sam hadn't been able to change the deputy's mind. After hearing about his daughter being threatened, Sam couldn't help feeling bad for the guy.

Granted, the cop should have gotten the help he needed to get off using the pain meds and then he should have gone to the authorities right away when the mayor forced him into a life of crime. All Sam could do now was to pray that the little girl and her grandmother would be safe from the long reach of the cartel.

"Ranger Hayward?" Rachel's voice had him turning toward her. "I need to talk to you."

Hesitantly, he crossed the parking lot to where she stood, still cuffed, beside a squad. "Ma'am, you have the right to remain silent," he said. "And the right to an attorney."

"I don't care about that." She lifted her chin. "I want you to know the truth."

He hesitated, unwilling to do this here. "You really need to wait for your lawyer," he tried again.

"I waive my rights. I'm afraid Mayor Beaumont and Doug Granger will get away with this." She sniffled again, glancing at her dead husband. "I want you to know exactly what happened. This all started when I noticed a slew of anonymous donations in relatively small amounts, anywhere from five hundred to a thousand dollars coming into Beaumont's campaign."

Just as they'd thought. "From the cartel?"

"Yes. And Hank George had expressed his concerns about the construction company using so many hired hands and goods from Mexico, so he got rid of the contract. Next thing I know, he's dead and Roy Carlton was arrested for his murder."

"We already figured out that much," Sam said. "But what about Jeff Abbott?"

"That was awful," she said. "Jeff visited Roy

in jail, then showed up at the office to tell the mayor—you know he's Jeff's stepfather—about the proof Roy had hidden at the ranch of his innocence. That caused a huge fight. A few weeks later, I was told to contact my husband. That was when Mayor Beaumont told Joe to eliminate the threat." She swallowed hard. "He didn't want to, but Beaumont said the cartel would find Ashley and kill her. So he did that and helped Roy Carlton escape, too so that it would be easier to eliminate him. Joe killed Abbott and left him on the ranch, hoping to implicate Ms. Lynch so that he could get in the house to find the evidence Roy claimed was there. Only Roy surprised him by showing up to kidnap his own son, apparently to get access to the evidence too. Joe said he found Roy hiding in the bushes and dragged him out of there, forcing him to talk. That's when he learned about the evidence Roy had hidden in his son's stuffed animal."

It was all starting to make sense now. "So he took shots at Mari and Theo, trying to get them out of the way."

She grimaced. "I think he only wanted to scare them. Joe wasn't heartless. He didn't want to kill anyone, especially not a young woman and her son. Beaumont made him do it!"

"Okay, I hear you." Sam pulled his phone from his pocket to call his boss. "We need to arrest Beaumont, send teams to both City Hall and his private residence. We have a witness that will testify against him."

"Got it," Owens agreed.

"Are my mother and daughter safe?" Rachel's gaze clung to his. "Will you let me know?"

"It's going to take some time for the rangers to reach San Antonio," he said. "But I will make sure someone lets you know when they're in protective custody."

"Thank you." Rachel closed her eyes and hung her head for a moment. "We shouldn't have let things go this far," she whispered.

That was a massive understatement, but he didn't say anything. Rachel Strawn had already learned the hard way about how bad choices could result in even worse consequences.

He turned away, about to head into the motel to check on Mari and Theo, when he saw two officers kneeling beside Joe Strawn.

"I don't understand why he wasn't wearing a vest," the first officer on the scene said with a frown. "It's a standard part of the uniform."

"Suicide by cop," his female partner said with a shrug. "Wouldn't be the first time."

Sam went still as he once again remembered the resignation in Joe's eyes. The way Joe had wanted him to shoot.

So much death and destruction for what? Money? Power?

He shook his head in frustration. After crossing to the motel room door, he rapped on it with his knuckle. "Mari? Theo? Are you okay?"

There was no response for a moment, then the door opened barely an inch. "Sam?"

"Yes." He waited for Mari to open the door wider. He stepped inside, noticing that she carried Theo with her. The little boy looked at him warily. "Everything okay?"

"We'd like to go home." Mari didn't meet his gaze. "As soon as possible."

He didn't like the sound of that. She was already pulling away from him, acting as if they were barely acquaintances. As if they'd never hugged, kissed or supported each other.

She was ending things before they'd had a chance to develop into something more.

"I promise to take you and Theo home as soon as we know Mayor Beaumont has been taken into custody." He gestured to the bed. "Sit down, Mari. Rachel told me everything and has agreed to testify against Beaumont. You and Theo don't have to be afraid anymore."

"She did?" Mari looked surprised. "I thought she was worried about her daughter?"

"Tucker and Jackson are headed to get her mother and daughter now." He glanced at his watch, surprised more than an hour had passed. "They should be in San Antonio any minute."

"So it really is over," she whispered.

"Yes. We'll get Beaumont into custody and that will be the end of it." He hesitated, then added, "With Beaumont in jail, and hopefully spilling the beans on the cartel members he was working for, I doubt they'll stick around. With the operation being blown open, they have no reason to come after you and Theo."

"Are you sure about that?" She finally met his gaze. "What about revenge?"

"Beaumont is the one who is at risk of being hurt in revenge from the cartel," he said softly. "Not you and Theo. Unfortunately, your ex-husband is the one who pulled you into this. According to Rachel, her husband is the one who fired shots at you, on Beaumont's orders. And Strawn killed Abbott and your ex, too. They probably wanted Roy to lead them to his hidden evidence, which is exactly what he did."

She closed her eyes for a moment, then nodded. She looked stronger now. "I understand. But we'd still like to go home."

"Soon." He sent Owens a text about letting him know when Beaumont was arrested. Then he sat beside Mari and Theo on the edge of the bed. "I'd like to sleep in your living room for a few days, just to be safe."

Her head snapped around to face him. "You just said we were safe," she accused.

"Yes, but I can't just leave." He hesitated, trying to put his thoughts and feelings into words. "I care about you and Theo. I want to spend some time with you. This way, I can make sure your windows are all repaired."

"I—don't think that's a good idea." She turned away, shifting Theo in her lap.

His stomach dropped. "Why not? No pressure, I only want to help."

"Mr. Sam, I want my toys," Theo said interrupting the moment.

"I know, we'll leave soon." He searched her gaze. "Mari? What's going on?"

"Theo is afraid of…" She gestured to the empty holster on his belt. He'd handed his weapon over to the responding officers as they'd be tasked with investigating the shooting. "He was very scared with everything that happened."

"I see." He turned and knelt in front of Theo. "Theo, I'm sorry you were frightened. But remember how I promised to keep you and your mom safe?"

Theo nodded.

"Well, to do that I had to fire my gun. But then I gave it to the police officers, see?" He made a point of showing his empty holster. "You don't have to be afraid anymore. Because I love your mom and I will do everything in my power to keep you and your mom safe."

"Love?" Mari repeated, her eyes widening.

He looked from Theo up into Mari's wide, green eyes. "Love," he repeated. "I fell in love with you and Theo, too. But I know you don't feel the same way. I only ask that you allow me to stay at the ranch long enough to ensure the window repairs are finished. After that, I'll leave. If that's what you want," he amended. Because in truth, he didn't want to go away from her.

He wanted to stay and celebrate the new year with her. And Theo's birthday, too.

But that wasn't up to him. He wouldn't push himself into Mari's life.

"Oh, Sam." Her eyes filled with tears. "That's so sweet. To be honest, I have fallen in love with you, too."

"Thank the Lord Jesus," he said in a heartfelt prayer. "Mari, I love you more than anything. Just give me a chance to show you how much."

His phone dinged with a text from Owens. It was brief.

We got him.

Hallelujah, he thought. Beaumont was in custody.

"I guess we'll both have to figure out how to make things work," she said with a frown. "You travel a lot and I can't leave the ranch."

"We'll make it work." He bent to give Theo a

kiss on his head, then rose to his feet, drawing Mari up, too. Bringing both Mari and Theo into his embrace, he dropped a chaste kiss on Mari's cheek. "Love always finds a way."

"I know." To his surprise, she lifted up to kiss him on the lips. "Thank you for everything, Sam. For saving our lives and for being here when we needed you the most."

"Thank you, Mari." He frowned. "Although I was not happy you charged Doug Granger like an angry bull. Marsh would have taken care of him."

"I was so mad when he turned the gun on you," she admitted sheepishly. "I acted without thinking."

He sighed and hugged her and Theo close. "Well, don't do that again."

"I won't." She grimaced. "I'm still sore from the tackle."

He'd loved the way she cared enough to risk her life, but absolutely didn't want her anywhere near danger ever again. "Beaumont is in custody." He held her gaze. "It's over for good, Mari."

"That's wonderful." Her smile lit up her whole face. "Let's go home, Sam."

Home. The word resonated deep within. And he knew if he had his way, he wouldn't leave Mari and Theo ever again.

SEVENTEEN

New Year's Eve

The past few days had been wonderful. Mari couldn't believe how easily Sam fit into their lives. Oh, she knew this was a temporary reprieve, because Sam would still have to travel with his job, but during the time they had together, Sam was an equal partner. They shared a camaraderie she'd never experienced before.

When she'd suggested grilled steaks, potatoes and salads for dinner, he'd immediately volunteered to cook. And she wasn't sure how, but he'd gotten her windows replaced within twenty-four hours of their return to the ranch, too. The routine ranch chores didn't take nearly as long with Sam's helping hand. She had no doubt that her father would have loved Sam, which was the exact opposite of how he'd felt toward Roy.

Theo still had the occasional nightmare, but with Sam sleeping on the living room sofa, one of them was quickly able to help soothe Theo's fears.

"Can I stay up to see the New Year?" Theo asked when they'd finished eating.

"You can try," Mari agreed. "But it's okay if you fall asleep because we can celebrate the New Year in the morning, too. Don't forget, day two is your birthday. You don't want to be sleepy on your birthday, right?"

"Right." That seemed to satisfy him.

Sam met her gaze across the kitchen, and the promise of a new year kiss in his gaze made her blush.

He'd been so sweet, she sometimes pinched herself to make sure she wasn't dreaming.

"I heard from my boss yesterday while I was out shopping." Sam's tone was casual, but his gaze had turned serious.

"Oh?" She mentally braced herself. "About Beaumont?"

He nodded. "Beaumont gave up the cartel members he knew by name in exchange for a lesser sentence." He paused, then added, "Unfortunately, he was found dead in his cell the following morning. Apparently, the cartel has members inside the prison."

She sucked in a quick breath. "That's horrible."

"Yes. But we have issued several arrest warrants for those members. We'll continue keeping Marion and Ashley in protective custody and the federal marshals are working to get Marion, Ashley and Rachel new identities so they can start over. We know Roy spoke to Abbott shortly before his escape was arranged, so that part of Rachel's story pans out, too. And Longhorn Construction is out of business for good." He smiled. "I suspect the cartel members will head back to Mexico rather than risk being caught."

That was good news, although she still couldn't believe so many people had lost their lives over this. Then again, each of those involved had made a choice.

Bad choices. And she couldn't help but be relieved that Roy wasn't around to pose a threat any longer.

"I guess all we can do is to pray," she murmured.

"Yes," he agreed.

She joined Sam at the sink to finish the dishes. Then they all headed into the living room. She was doubly glad now that she still had her brightly lit tree. Mari was about to sit on the sofa, urging Sam to join her, when he took Theo's hand.

"Are you ready?" Sam asked Theo.

Her son nodded, looking excited. Then he turned to face her. "Mom, Sam asked me and I said yes."

"Yes, to what?" She was confused, but Sam just chuckled.

"He forgot the first part," Sam said with a wry grin. "Remember Theo? We practiced this morning. I asked you if I could marry your mom and you said yes."

"Yes!" Theo jumped up and down with excitement. "I said yes!"

She laughed, tears of joy pricking her eyes. She met Sam's gaze and her heart filled with joy.

"Ah, Mari. I love you so much." Sam pulled out a small ring box featuring a beautiful, shiny diamond ring. "Will you please marry me?"

"Yes, Sam. I would love to marry you." She let him put the ring on her finger then jumped up to hug him. They kissed, then he bent to lift Theo up so he could be a part of their embrace.

"Happy New Year, Mari and Theo," he said in a husky voice. It wasn't even close to midnight, but that didn't matter.

"Happy New Year, Sam." She kissed him again, then nestled her head into his shoulder. With God's love and grace enveloping them, she couldn't imagine a better way to start the new year.

And their new life together.

* * * * *

*Available now from Love Inspired Suspense!
Find more great reads at
www.LoveInspired.com.*

Dear Reader,

Thanks so much for reading Mari and Sam's story in *Texas Kidnapping Target*! I hope you enjoyed the first book in my Texas Ranger series. Please know, I wrote this story before the wildfires swept across Texas and I will continue to keep all of you in my prayers as those of you who were impacted recover from your loss.

I'm truly blessed to have wonderful readers like you. And I've had so much fun introducing Sam's fellow Texas Rangers, who will each get their own story. You won't want to miss a single one.

I adore hearing from my readers! I can be found through my website at laurascottbooks. com, via Facebook at Facebook.com/LauraScottBooks, Instagram at Instagram.com/laurascottbooks/, and X, formerly known as Twitter, @laurascottbooks.

You may want to take a moment to sign up for my monthly newsletter to learn about my new book releases, especially my next Texas Ranger story. And all subscribers receive a free novella not available for purchase on any platform.

Until next time,
Laura Scott